Cindi Myers is the author of more than fifty novels. When she's not crafting new romance plots, she enjoys skiing, gardening, cooking, crafting and daydreaming. A lover of small-town life, she lives with her husband and two spoiled dogs in the Colorado mountains.

Stranded with the Suspect

CINDI MYERS

MILLS & BOON

First published in Great Britain 2018
by Mills & Boon, an imprint of HarperCollins*Publishers*
1 London Bridge Street, London, SE1 9GF

Large Print edition 2018

© 2018 Cynthia Myers

ISBN: 978-0-263-07768-1

MIX
Paper from
responsible sources
FSC™ C007454

This book is produced from independently certified
FSC™ paper to ensure responsible forest management.
For more information visit www.harpercollins.co.uk/green.

Printed and bound in Great Britain
by CPI Group (UK) Ltd, Croydon, CR0 4YY

For Deann

Chapter One

"I'm sorry, we don't have any messages for you, Ms. Daniels. I promise to put any calls or other communications through to your room at once. Is there anything else I can do for you?" The desk clerk at the Brown Palace Hotel smiled as she spoke, as if she really was concerned that Andi have everything she needed.

"No. Thank you." Andi tried to return the smile, but it wasn't something she was used to doing anymore. The past year hadn't given her much to smile about.

"Did you enjoy your visit to our spa this morning?" the clerk asked, after a quick glance at her computer screen, which no doubt showed every spa treatment, room service meal and other amenity Andi had enjoyed during her stay at one of Denver's oldest luxury hotels.

"Yes, it was lovely." Everything about the Brown Palace was lovely, from the richly patterned carpet beneath her feet to the stained-glass skylights in the main lobby. Towering fresh flower arrangements and elegant artwork shared space with photographs of the many celebrated personages who had stayed at the hotel, from the Beatles to US presidents. But none of it impressed Andi. For one thing, she had seen it all too many times before, when she stayed here with her father, Senator Pete Matheson.

That seemed a lifetime ago. Now all of this—the opulence and grand sense of history—wasn't her world anymore. She craved simplicity over elegance, reality more than comfort. This felt so phony.

"If you need anything at all, please let me know, Ms. Daniels," the clerk said.

Andi nodded and turned from the desk. Her name wasn't even Daniels—it was Matheson. But Daniel Metwater had thought it amusing to register her under a variant of his Christian name when he had brought her here three days ago. He was supposed to have contacted her before now, to let her know he was coming to get her and take her home.

She reached up and put her hand over the pendant at her neck, the rose-cut diamond in the old-fashioned gold setting a comforting weight at the base of her throat. Daniel didn't know that she had taken it before she left to come to Denver, but after all, he had promised it to her baby, so why shouldn't she have it now? If he asked about it when he arrived, she would tell him she had been keeping it safe for him. He might not be pleased with that explanation at first, but he would come around. Daniel wanted her to be happy.

She waited for the elevator, her ankles swollen, feet hurting. Absently, she rubbed at the bulge of her abdomen, the baby kicking inside her. She tried to imagine what the little one looked like right now, recalling pictures in the tattered copy of *What to Expect When You're Expecting* that one of the women in camp had loaned her. She had no idea if she was carrying a boy or a girl. It didn't matter—she would be happy with either. Part of her was anxious for the child's arrival. Another part of her wanted to put it off as long as possible. She hadn't seen a doctor since the public clinic had confirmed her pregnancy months ago, so she had no idea of her due date. But the other women in camp had assured her that the baby would come out when it was ready, and that she would be ready then, also.

Since she wasn't ready for the birth, the baby must not be either, which was reassuring in a way. She didn't want to have her child alone in this city that no longer felt familiar to her. She wanted to be back in the camp in the wilderness in southwest Colorado, with the women attending her and the men waiting outside, chanting for her and the baby's health.

"Ms. Matheson? Andi Matheson?"

She turned toward the speaker before she could stop herself. A lean, athletic man with a blond goatee smiled at her. "So good to see you again," he said, with just a hint of a foreign accent. Austrian? Russian?

"I… I'm sorry. You must have me confused with someone else." She turned to face the elevator once more, but she could feel his eyes on her.

He stepped closer, brushing against her arm. "Oh, but I am sure I am right. I would never forget such a beautiful woman."

She said nothing, teeth clenched, willing the elevator doors to open so she could make her escape.

"You are living with the evangelist, Daniel Metwater, now, are you not?" the man asked.

Daniel wasn't an evangelist. Not in the sense most people used the word. He was a prophet and a teacher.

The man touched her arm. "I would very much like to meet your boyfriend. Perhaps you could arrange it, no?"

She jerked away. The gilded doors of the elevator opened and she hurried inside. The man started to follow, but a dark-haired man shoved him out of the way and slipped in after her, immediately hitting the button to close the doors. "What floor?" he asked, his back to her.

"Fourteenth," she said, still shaken from the encounter with the blond.

He pressed the button for fourteen, then turned to face her. She gasped as she recognized his face, and pressed her back against the railing on the inside of the elevator car. "What are you doing here?" she asked.

The vertical line between his dark brows deepened as he frowned at her. "I'm not going to hurt you," he said.

She wasn't afraid of him. Not exactly. Officer Simon Woolridge wore his disdain of her and the other members of the family she belonged to on his face for all to see, especially his contempt for the man who led them, their Prophet, Daniel Metwater, but he had never given Andi reason to be afraid of him. He had never tried to befriend her the way some of the members of his organization, the Ranger Brigade, had. After a lifetime of dealing with frauds and posers, she could appreciate that kind of honesty.

"Why are you here?" she asked again. "Is something wrong? Has something happened to the Prophet?"

The elevator door opened and Simon touched her elbow. "Let's go to your room, where we can talk."

He walked beside her to her room at the end of the hall, a tall, commanding presence at her right elbow. She was used to seeing him in uniform, but today he wore jeans and a black Western shirt that emphasized his broad shoulders and narrow waist. The clothes made him seem less familiar and more…intriguing. She hadn't bothered to look much past the uniform before, but now she was aware of him as a man most women would give a second—or a third—look to. He waited while she slipped her card key from her purse, slid it in the lock and opened the door. Then he followed her inside.

She braced herself for him to make a disparaging remark about her luxurious suite, a sharp contrast to the tent she had been living in since she had joined Daniel Metwater and his followers five months previously. But he only gave the room a cursory glance before turning to her. "How are you feeling?" he asked.

The question caught her off guard. "I'm fine," she said automatically.

His gaze swept over her, his dark eyes intense, making her want to cover herself, even though she was fully dressed. He reminded her of a sleek cat, preparing to pounce on its prey. "You look pale," he said. "Your ankles are swollen and you keep arching your back, as if it hurts."

She put a hand to her lower back, which did ache, as did her swollen feet. She didn't know whether to be flattered he had noticed so much in such a short time, or to be unnerved by his scrutiny. "I'm fine," she said again.

"You're a lousy liar. Who was the man you were talking to by the elevator downstairs?"

"I don't know."

"He acted as if he knew you."

Yes. And that had been unsettling. "He knew who I was," she said. "He called me by my name—my real name."

"I heard him ask about Metwater."

"Yes. He wanted to meet him. Maybe he was simply a fan." Yes, that was probably it. The Prophet attracted many followers wherever he went.

Simon turned away from her to prowl the room like a restless predator. "Metwater must be doing pretty well siphoning money off his followers," he said. "If he can afford to hide you away here."

There was the cynicism she had been expecting. "I'm not hiding," she said. "And the Prophet has money of his own. He inherited it from his father."

Simon paused in his circuit of the room and looked back at her. "Then why does he need your money?"

Andi didn't answer.

"You signed the agreement, didn't you?" Simon asked. "The one that gives Daniel Metwater all your assets—now and in the future, as long as you remain with him."

"The money goes to the Family," she said. "We pool our resources so that no one has more than anyone else."

"The money goes into Daniel Metwater's personal bank account. I have the records, if you don't believe me."

The Rangers had no business looking into the private affairs of the Prophet, though of course, they thought their badges gave them the right. "He decides the best use of the funds for the Family," she said.

"I guess this week, stashing you in a suite in the Brown Palace was the best use of the funds."

Again, she said nothing. He had obviously made up his mind. And what business was it of his how the Family spent their money? She opened her mouth to ask him, but he cut her off.

"Whose idea was it to come here?" he asked her.

"The Prophet's."

"He wanted you here so that you couldn't tell us anything we could use against him," Simon said. "But it's too late for that now. We already have everything we need to put him away."

"Are you saying you arrested him?" She tried to keep the alarm out of her voice, but failed.

For months, the Rangers had been harassing Daniel Metwater and his followers. The Family, as they called themselves, got the blame for every crime that occurred on the public lands the Ranger Brigade patrolled.

"When was the last time you heard from him?" Simon asked.

"I haven't heard anything from him since he brought me here three days ago," she said. "Why? Where is he? What have you done to him?"

"We haven't done anything. We don't know where he is." Simon's eyes met hers, black and hard as coal. "I was hoping you did."

She shook her head and sank onto the sofa, fearful her legs would no longer support her. "What's happened? Why are you looking for him?"

"We found your friend Starfall's baby."

"Hunter!" Fear clogged her throat. Her tentmate's child had disappeared from camp two days before Metwater drove Andi to Denver. Starfall had accused the Prophet of taking her child, but Andi knew that couldn't be true. "Is he okay? Where was he?"

"He's fine. He was with a couple of guys named Smith. Two brothers. Sound familiar?"

She shook her head, relief flooding her. "Then you know Daniel didn't take Hunter," she said. "Why are you still looking for him when you know he's innocent?"

"The Smith brothers told us Daniel Metwater paid them to take Starfall's baby," Simon said. "Metwater said he wanted to teach her a lesson."

Andi shook her head. "No. He wouldn't do something like that."

"Then why did he kidnap Starfall and try to kill her? He tried to kill Ethan Reynolds, the Ranger who was trying to help her, too."

"You're lying. The Prophet would never do anything like that. He promotes peace."

Simon stood over her, his shadow falling across her face, his bulk making her feel even smaller. "Why are you defending him?" he demanded. "What has he done for you but take your money and sleep with other women?"

She cringed at the words. "He's trying to teach me not to be possessive." Wanting the Prophet of their people all to herself was her personal failing, one she struggled with.

"A truly good man wouldn't treat you this way," Simon said, his voice gentler. "He would cherish you and protect you, not lie to you and use you."

"You don't know what you're talking about."

His expression hardened. "Maybe not. But I know you're in danger if you don't get away from him."

"Danger?" The word shocked her out of her

despair. She sat up straighter. "What kind of danger?"

"Daniel Metwater is running for his life right now. Every law enforcement agency in the country is hunting for him," Simon said. "He knows sooner or later we're going to catch him. When we do, he doesn't want you around to testify against him."

"I would never testify against him," she said, horrified at the idea.

"You're not married to him. You can be compelled to tell what you know."

"But I don't know anything."

"I think you do," Simon said. "You're closer to Daniel Metwater than anyone. You may not realize the significance of the information, but it's something big enough that he took care to hide you away here, under an assumed name."

"If that's true and he's so terrible, why didn't

he just kill me?" she asked. "That's apparently the kind of man you think he is."

Simon's expression didn't change. "He has to keep you alive until your twenty-fifth birthday, when your trust comes under your control. If you die after that, the money all goes to Daniel Metwater—am I right?"

He was, though she had no intention of confirming this. "The Prophet would never harm me," she said.

"I'll bet Starfall thought the same thing, until he beat her and stole her baby."

Andi pressed her hands against her belly, feeling the child shift inside her. "You need to leave," she said.

"I'll go for now," he said. "But I won't be far away." He headed toward the door. "I have a feeling Metwater is going to come back for you, and when he does, he'll find me waiting."

He left, closing the door firmly behind him.

She stared after him, rage and fear and sickness swirling through her. Simon Woolridge was a horrible man. How could he make such terrible accusations against a man who spoke words of peace and caring? Daniel Metwater had saved her, and so many others.

Simon was a hard, abrasive cop who had no concern for her or her feelings.

But Daniel Metwater, despite all his goodness, had lied to her more than once. As far as she knew, Simon had never lied to her, even when telling the truth hurt.

Chapter Two

Simon prowled the hallway outside Andi's room, immune to the appeal of well-upholstered chairs and elegant chandeliers. He viewed the hotel like a battleground, noting positions from which to mount an offensive, and the many places a fugitive might hide.

His conversation with Andi hadn't gone as he had hoped. He had meant to come down hard on her, to insist that she come with him to a shelter or another place of safety. But one look at her beautiful, weary face had melted his resolve. Maybe it was better for her and her baby if she stayed here, where she would at least be comfortable. He would guard her and wait.

Metwater was going to come for her; Simon was sure of it. The man preached poverty and the simple life to his followers, but he had used the very people who depended on him to amass assets in excess of sixty-eight million dollars. And that was only the accounts Simon had managed to locate. There was probably more stashed elsewhere.

But he was a fugitive on the run now, his bank accounts frozen and unavailable to him. He would need money to leave the country, to run out of the reach of US law. Andi had money, and Metwater could be confident she would give it to him. All he had to do was get to her. A different type of man might have gotten by on wits and cunning alone, but Metwater was used to paying his way out of trouble.

He was the son of a man who had made a

fortune manufacturing plastics in Chicago. He had a twin brother, David, who had reportedly embezzled hundreds of thousands of dollars from the family business before Metwater Senior's death. Without his dad to reign him in, David had really gone off the rails, racking up gambling debts, dabbling in the drug trade and getting in deep with the Russian mob. He had died under mysterious circumstances, supposedly killed by organized crime members he had tried to double-cross.

Meanwhile, Daniel kept on managing the family business, serving on the boards of various charities and cleaning up the mess his brother made. David's death, he told the press, cut him deeply, to the point where he sold the family business and took to the road, preaching peace and poverty to a growing list of followers, who eventually followed him to the public lands of Colorado, where they set up camp in the Rangers' jurisdiction.

The good twin and the bad twin. A classic cliché. Simon didn't buy it. He figured Daniel had been every bit as corrupt as his twin, but managed to hide it better. Nobody was the saint the press made Daniel out to be.

Simon knew a few real saints—nuns who lived real vows of poverty and worked to save children in border-town slums, doctors who used their own money to fund clinics for the indigent, police officers who faced down corruption and paid the ultimate price when they were assassinated for refusing to look the other way.

But Simon was no saint. Working for Immigration and Customs Enforcement, he had sent widows and orphans back to uncertain futures and poverty because they had the bad luck to be born on the wrong side of the border. He didn't believe in mercy for those who broke the law, and he had little patience for whiners and weaklings.

And he knew there was a special place in hell for men like Daniel Metwater, who took advantage of the lost and lonely.

Beautiful Andi Matheson was a little of both. She had the kind of ethereal beauty that drew the eye. The first time Simon had seen the blonde there in Metwater's camp, he had a hard time not staring. She had been born into privilege and by all accounts was a spoiled socialite who had never been denied anything—all reasons enough for him to dislike her, which he had been prepared to do.

Then he had looked into those sapphire eyes, and the hurt and fear in them had hit him like a sucker punch. Stripped of her beauty-queen gowns and protected privilege, he had seen her for the lost, struggling soul she was. From that moment on, Simon had appointed himself Andi's guardian. Which is why he patrolled the hallways and public areas of the hotel, alert to anything that might signal danger.

He was torn between the desire to station himself outside Andi's door, and the need to find and question the man who had spoken to her at the elevator. Simon sensed a threat from that man. If he could deal with the stranger, then he could focus on Metwater.

In the hotel bar, The Ship Tavern, he spotted a familiar blond head—the man who had approached Andi outside the elevators. He entered the bar and was immediately engulfed by a wave of noise—a dozen conversations rising over the blare of two TVs and the clink of glasses. The gleam of brass—brass railings, brass light fixtures, brass ornaments on the wall—caught and reflected back the light from old-fashioned ship's lanterns and faceted chan-

deliers. Simon squeezed past a shapely bru-
nette in a sequined cocktail gown. She smiled
warmly and looked him up and down. "Hi,
handsome," she breathed.

He ignored her and continued on until he
reached the bar, and eased in beside the blond
man, who immediately turned to see who had
joined him. Simon nodded in greeting. The
blond returned the nod, and gave no indication that he recognized Simon. "What can I
get you?" the bartender asked.

"Fat Tire," Simon said. When the bartender
had walked away, Simon turned once more to
the blond. "I saw you talking to Andi Matheson earlier," he said. He seldom wasted time
with subtlety. In his experience, a direct con-
frontation was more likely to catch people off
guard.

The blond tensed, one hand slipping inside
his jacket. "Who are you?"

"Are you going to shoot me right here in this bar because I made a simple remark?" Simon kept his voice even as he turned to accept the beer from the bartender, who flicked a glance at the blond.

The blond brought his hand back out in the open and nodded to the bartender. "My friend thinks he's so funny," he said, his English very good, but definitely with a hint of a Russian accent.

The blond waited until the bartender had walked away before he spoke again, keeping his hands outside his coat. "Who are you?" he asked again.

"I'm a friend of Ms. Matheson's," Simon said. "Who are you?"

"You're the man in the elevator." Understanding lit his eyes.

"Who are you and what do you want with her?" Simon asked.

"I am also a friend."

"That's not what she says. She says she never saw you before."

"She doesn't remember." He sipped his drink—something dark and thick in a small glass. "It was at a party, with a lot of people."

"When? Where?"

"Why are you so interested?"

"It's my business to be interested."

The blond studied Simon more closely. He tensed again, eyes narrowed. "You're a cop," he said.

Simon didn't deny or confirm, but met the blond's glare with a hard look of his own.

"I don't like cops," the blond said.

"I don't like people who bother Ms. Matheson. She said you asked her about Daniel Metwater."

The blond contemplated the liquid in the

glass. "Her boyfriend. He's putting her up here, isn't he?"

"What makes you think that?"

"I have a connection at the front desk." He cut his eyes to Simon, his expression wary. "Are you after her for something—or is it Metwater you want?"

"Right now, I'm interested in you."

"I'm a man having a drink in a public bar." He drained his glass and set it down on the bar with a hard *thunk*. He pulled a heavy gold money clip from his pocket, peeled off a twenty and laid it on the bar. "Good night."

"Leave Ms. Matheson alone," Simon said.

"Watch your back," the blond said softly, but loud enough for Simon to hear.

Simon started after him, only to be blocked by a group of men and women who pushed toward the bar. By the time he got free, he reached the door just in time to see the blond pushing through the glass doors of the hotel lobby to the street.

Simon returned to the bar and paid for his beer, then walked back into the lobby. A quick scan satisfied him that the blond hadn't returned. But Simon had added the Russian to the short list of people who might be a danger to Andi.

He made his way back to the fourteenth floor and the room two doors down from Andi's. His bosses were going to scream when they got the bill for the suite, but it couldn't be helped. If Daniel Metwater—or the Russian—tried to get to Andi, they would have to get past Simon first.

SIMON'S VISIT HAD banished all hope Andi had of resting. Not that she had been sleeping much lately anyway. She missed having other women around to talk to—that had been one of the best things about joining the Family. An only child, she had never realized how comforting it could be to have other women around you—sisters who understood your concerns and were always willing to listen or offer advice. Casual acquaintances you didn't live with could never understand you as well as family. A check of the clock showed it was only eight thirty, so she dialed the number for her former tentmate at the Family's camp, Starfall. She would have to remember to call her Michelle, now that she had left the group and decided to go by her birth name once more.

"Hello?" Michelle answered.

"Hi. It's Andi."

"What do you want?" Michelle's voice wasn't exactly angry, but it wasn't friendly either.

Andi grimaced. She had forgotten that the two of them had argued the last time they had spoken. "I heard they found Hunter safe," she said. "I wanted to tell you how glad I am about that." Michelle must have been half-crazy with worry when her little boy disappeared.

"No thanks to Daniel Metwater," Michelle said. "He was the one who hired the guys who kidnapped him. And then Metwater tried to kill me. He tried to kill Ethan too."

So it was true. Not that Andi had really doubted Simon's words. "I heard," she said. "I'm sorry."

"Who told you about it? You're not with Metwater now, are you?"

"No, no. I haven't seen or spoken to him. Simon Woolridge told me. He's one of the officers with the Ranger Brigade."

"I know Simon. When did you talk to him?"

"A little while ago. He came to Denver—I guess he's hoping he'll catch the Prophet when he comes to pick me up at the hotel. But I don't think he's coming. Why would he risk it?"

"Besides the fact that he thinks he can get away with anything?" Michelle asked.

"Why did he try to kill you?" Andi asked. "Why would he want to kidnap Hunter? None of that makes sense to me."

"I don't know," Michelle said. "Most of what he said didn't make sense—but Ethan thinks it's because I know something that could get him into trouble."

"Ethan is the officer who was helping you?" Andi asked.

"Yes. He's been great." Michelle's voice softened, her tone almost wistful. "I can't believe how great he's been."

"What does he think you know that could hurt the Prophet?" Andi asked.

"I wish I knew what it was—I'd shout it from the rooftops."

"Simon says he thinks I must know something that could hurt Daniel, too," Andi said. "That's why he hid me away here in Denver."

"So, what do you know?"

"Nothing. I swear. I can't think of anything."

"You spent the most time with him and were closest to him," Michelle said. "I'll bet you saw a lot of things you shouldn't have."

"No." In spite of all the time they'd spent together, she really didn't know much at all about Daniel Metwater. He had kept her ignorant, changing the subject whenever she asked about the past or his plans for the future, or even what he did in the hours she wasn't with him. She knew only what he wanted her to know, and that wasn't anything beyond his public image as a sincere, wise teacher and leader.

"Stay away from him, Andi," Michelle said. "He wants people to think he's good and has their best interests at heart, but that's not true."

"I'll be careful," Andi said.

"Stick with Simon," Michelle said. "The Rangers had Metwater figured out a long time ago. I wish now we had listened to them."

"It's a little strange, hearing you, of all people, talking about trusting the cops," Andi said. The Prophet had always taught that law enforcement officers were not their friends, and Michelle, who had apparently had her share of run-ins with the police, had agreed wholeheartedly with this assessment.

Michelle laughed. "And now I'm in love with one. I can hardly believe it myself."

"I'm glad things are working out so well for you," Andi said, ignoring the stab of jealousy that lanced through her. Michelle sounded so happy. As if she lived in some alternate universe different from the one Andi occupied. It didn't even seem possible to be that happy in her world.

"Take care of yourself," Michelle said. "And

keep in touch. Let me know when your baby is born."

"I will." They said goodbye and Andi hung up the phone. She had hoped talking to a friend would soothe her, but the conversation had only reinforced the reasons she had to be worried and afraid. All this emotional upheaval couldn't be good for the baby. She needed to find a way to stay calm.

She phoned room service and ordered a cup of warm milk. That had been her mother's remedy when Andi struggled to get to sleep as a girl. She set down the phone, tears pricking her eyes at the memory of her mother. Cancer had taken her almost ten years ago. Everything had changed after that—Andi's father had become more focused on his political career, more concerned with power and prestige than with his daughter, except when she could be an asset to his image.

If her mother had lived, maybe things would have been different. Maybe Andi wouldn't have fallen for her father's bodyguard—a man who turned out to be married. Already pregnant, Andi had discovered the bodyguard's deception and her father's corruption. Wanting to escape the dishonesty and shallowness of her life, she had found solace in the teachings of Daniel Metwater. She was sure he was a man she could respect and love, and she hated men like Simon Woolridge for making her doubt her beliefs.

Now Michelle was telling her Simon was right, and she didn't know what to think. Had her judgment really been so poor? Or was Daniel Metwater extremely gifted in deceiving people?

A knock on the door disturbed her thoughts, and she checked the peephole and recognized the livery of the hotel staff. Relieved, she opened the door, only to find herself shoved backward into the room.

Daniel Metwater tossed the tray with the cup of milk aside and grabbed Andi by the wrists. "We don't have much time," he said. "We have to get out of here."

Chapter Three

Simon paced the length of the hotel room, too unsettled to sit still. When he had booked the room, he had imagined using it as a base to keep an eye on Andi's suite, but the layout was all wrong. He couldn't see her door clearly from here, and the walls were too thick, the carpeting too plush, for him to hear anyone approaching.

Under other circumstances, he could have worked with hotel security to set up a surveillance camera to monitor her door. But that kind of thing took warrants—and it took time. Time Simon didn't have.

Metwater was running, and he was desperate. Maybe he would leave town, or even leave the country and forget about Andi altogether, but Simon didn't think so. For one thing, he didn't have the resources he would need to make a getaway. For another, he had already proven he didn't like loose ends or unfinished business. He had hidden Andi away here—or thought he had—when the Rangers began closing in. He didn't want the cops talking to her.

And Metwater would know that Andi's twenty-fifth birthday was only a few days away. Once her trust—several million dollars—passed to her, he could use his power over her to control the funds. A man as greedy as Metwater wouldn't want to pass up the opportunity to have that kind of money.

Simon had the Russian to consider too. He had seen the man leave the hotel, but he could have easily circled around and come back in through another entrance. Though the man hadn't directly threatened Andi, Simon couldn't shake the feeling that he was a danger to her.

Not on my watch, Simon thought, and stepped back into the hallway. He could station himself outside Andi's doorway as a guard, but Metwater would see him and avoid approaching. That might keep Andi safe, but it wouldn't trap Metwater. Simon wanted to stop the Prophet before he hurt anyone else. That meant staying hidden and getting the jump on him when he did approach.

He scanned the hallway, his gaze coming to rest on a recess that housed a decorative plant. A real plant, he noted as he squeezed in behind it, not a silk one. The space was cramped and uncomfortable, but he settled in as best he could, gun drawn, eyes focused on the doorway to Andi's room and the hallway leading up to it.

The events of the past two days dragged at him—the rescue of Hunter Munson, the search for Michelle and Ethan, their safe return and then the long drive to Denver to get to Andi before Metwater could reach her. He fought sleep by focusing on the Russian. Where did he fit into the picture? Metwater's twin brother had supposedly been murdered—rather, assassinated—by the *Bratva,* the Russian mob, though the Chicago police had never found enough evidence to formally charge anyone with the crime. The case was still open.

When Russians had shown up in Black Canyon of the Gunnison National Park and two people associated with them had ended up dead, Daniel Metwater had panicked and demanded protection from the Ranger Brigade, though he would never say why he thought the

Russians were after him. The Russians turned out to be part of a smuggling ring that was trying to move into the park, and not after Metwater at all, but the cool, sophisticated mask of the Prophet had slipped for those few days, allowing Simon to see how frightened he really was.

Did he know the blond Russian was asking about him—possibly looking for him? Or was the man, as he had said, merely someone who had met Andi before who wanted to renew the acquaintance? After all, she was a very attractive woman—her pregnancy didn't detract at all from her beauty.

The elevator opened and a man in hotel livery stepped out, carrying a tray. He moved past Simon without noticing him, head down, a bored employee on the late shift, with hours to go before he got off work. He approached the door and knocked, and after a moment it opened and he stepped inside.

Simon waited. One minute. Two. How long did it take to deliver a tray, collect the tip and leave? His heart started racing, anxiety knotting his stomach. Something about the waiter wasn't right. Something about the way he walked was a little too familiar. His blood went cold as he realized why.

He exploded from behind the plant and raced for Andi's room, praying he wasn't already too late.

GONE WAS THE SERENE, confident Prophet who had mesmerized Andi so. The man before her was unshaven and dirty beneath the clean clothes he must have taken from the real room service waiter, his hair greasy and smelling of sweat. She tried to pull out of his grasp. "Let go, you're hurting me!" she protested.

He released her, but his attitude didn't soften. "Call for a taxi. Tell the driver to meet you across the street, in front of the bank. What have you got that I can wear? And I need a scarf for my hair. I'll be your sister, visiting from Grand Junction."

"Daniel, wait! What's going on?"

"You're going to help me get out of here, that's what's going on," he said.

"What about Starfall, and that cop—Ethan? And Starfall's baby, Hunter? Did you really try to hurt them?" She hadn't meant to say anything about any of that, but the words tumbled out. Simon and Michelle had planted all these doubts in her head and she needed the Prophet to allay her fears.

"Who have you been talking to?" He turned on her, rage contorting his face, and before she could draw back he hit her, hard, snapping her head back and leaving her cheek stinging.

She gasped, tears filling her eyes. No one had ever hit her before—no one. "Shut up and get moving," Metwater said. "Or I'll make you wish you'd obeyed me when you had the chance."

He turned back toward the door, but it burst open. Simon Woolridge didn't hesitate; he hit Metwater hard, dropping him to his knees. He pulled flexi-cuffs from his belt and reached for the Prophet's wrist. "Daniel Metwater, you are under arrest."

Metwater shook his head and rose up with a roar, shoving Simon backward. Andi screamed.

"Get out of here!" Simon shouted at her. "Go to the lobby, where you'll be safe."

"No." She couldn't leave him. For that matter, she couldn't leave the Prophet. She had to stay and see how this played out.

Metwater lunged at Simon, swinging hard. Simon dodged the punch, but crashed into an end table, sending it toppling. The Tiffany-style lamp that had been sitting on it slid to the floor and shattered into a kaleidoscope of bright shards. Andi screamed again and looked around for anything she could use to defend herself. Simon staggered to his feet, reaching for the gun in the holster at his side. A vision of him shooting the Prophet filled her head. "No!" she sobbed, and started toward him.

He turned at the sound of her voice, which gave Metwater the opening he needed to grab Simon's arm, trying to get at the weapon. "Don't kill him!" Andi pleaded, not even sure which man she was defending now.

The men reeled away from her, grappling, and crashed into a second table, sending more fragile ornaments cascading to the floor. Glass crunched under her feet as she backed away. She spotted the telephone on the table at the end of the sofa. She should call someone. Not the police—they were looking for Daniel. But the front desk? Housekeeping, to clean up the mess?

Fighting back hysterical laughter, she reached for the phone, just as someone pounded on the door. "Hotel security!" boomed a man's voice. "What's going on in there?"

Daniel Metwater jerked his head toward the door. "Don't open it," he growled.

"Open the door!" Simon ordered.

"If you don't open up in five seconds, we're coming in!" the voice on the other side said.

Andi started toward the door. She had taken only two steps when Metwater rushed past her. She reeled away from him, but he scarcely noticed. He jerked open the door and, as two uniformed men rushed in, he ran past them and down the hall.

Simon tried to run after Metwater, but the two men who had just entered the room held him back. "What's going on here?" the first man, tall and broad-shouldered, demanded.

Simon, whose shirt was half out of his jeans and who was bleeding from his mouth, still managed to look dignified as he presented his credentials. "Agent Simon Woolridge, Ranger Brigade," he said. "The man who ran out of here is Daniel Metwater, a wanted fugitive." He tried to move past them again, but the men—who were dressed in the uniforms of hotel security—held him fast.

The first guard studied Simon's credentials for a long moment before returning them to Simon. "What's your fugitive doing in this hotel?" he asked.

"Probably getting away," Simon said, as he tucked the leather folder back into his pocket. He shoved past the two guards, who let him go this time. He rushed out the door, footsteps pounding down the hall.

"Ma'am, are you all right?" asked the second security guard, who was short but muscular.

She nodded, and pushed her hair out of her face. "I… I'm fine," she managed.

"We had a report of screams and crashing," said the second man. "Sounds of a struggle." He surveyed the broken glass and overturned tables. "Can you tell us what happened?"

She shook her head. What exactly *had* happened? Had the Prophet really hit her? Had he really threatened her? The violence was so unlike him. He would never want to hurt her, would he? "He burst in here, and he was terribly upset," she began. "He's desperate, I think. And afraid…"

Simon stepped into the room once more, breathing hard. "He got away," he said. "We'll need to block all the entrances and conduct a search of the entire hotel."

The two guards blinked at him. "We don't

have the authority to do something like that," the first man said.

"Don't you need a warrant or something?" the second man asked.

"Do you want to wait until he kills one of your guests before you do more than stand around twiddling your thumbs?" Simon snapped.

"I don't really think the Prophet would kill anyone," Andi protested.

"He could have killed you," Simon said. His eyes met hers, searing her with their anger. He turned back toward the security guards and she started to protest, but a sharp cry out of her own mouth cut off her words.

She cradled her abdomen and tried to brace herself against the sharp pain that tore through her. As she blinked back tears, she realized the three men were staring at her. Simon was the first to reach her side. "What is it?" he asked. "What's wrong?"

She shook her head. "I'm fine. Just…gas or something."

"She needs a doctor," Simon said, helping her to the sofa.

"We have a physician on call." The older security guard pulled out his phone and punched in some numbers.

"No. I'll be fi—" But another sharp pain cut off the words. Andi closed her eyes. She couldn't be going into labor. Not now. Not when so much was unsettled.

Simon took hold of her ankles and swung her feet up onto the sofa. "Lie back and close your eyes," he said. "Breathe deeply and try to relax." He had removed her shoes and was rubbing her feet. She ought to object, but it felt so good she couldn't force the words past her lips.

"What about your felon?" one of the security guards asked.

"His name is Daniel Metwater," Simon said. "Thirty-two years old. Six foot two inches, one-hundred sixty-five pounds, curly dark hair and eyes. Contact the police and alert the rest of your staff, but if you see him, don't try to deal with him yourself. He's dangerous and may be armed. But he has enough of a head start that he's probably already left the hotel."

"We'll get someone up here to clean up this mess once the doctor is done," one of the men said.

"It can wait until morning," Simon said. "I don't want any more strangers in here than necessary."

Andi kept her eyes closed and let herself drift. Simon's hands were warm, his fingers strong and soothing. Where had he learned to give a foot massage like that? As he dug his thumb into her aching arch, she had to bite back a moan. She may even have fallen asleep.

She wasn't sure how much time had passed when someone squeezed her hand. "Hello, Ms. Daniels," said a smooth, lightly accented voice. "I'm Dr. Johar. I understand you've been experiencing some discomfort."

She opened her eyes and stared into the face of a handsome, brown-skinned man. She looked past him, searching for Simon. "Where's Simon?" she asked.

"He's in the hallway, talking to the local cops." The older security guard stepped forward.

The police. They would be after Daniel. He wouldn't stand a chance now. She struggled into a sitting position. "I'm fine now," she said, hoping the words were true. She needed to talk to Simon, to plead with him not to be too hard on Daniel. Yes, he had hit her, but it must have been because he was out of his mind with fear. Ordinarily, he would never do anything like that.

Then Simon's face came into view, hovering over the doctor's left shoulder. "She had at least two moments of pain that were strong enough to make her cry out," Simon said. "I did what I could to help her relax."

"Are you her husband?" the doctor asked as he felt for Andi's pulse. "Or boyfriend?"

Andi waited to see how he would answer. "No," he said and turned away. "I'm a cop."

"Perhaps you would like to step away and give us a little privacy," the doctor said. "Ms. Daniels, would it be all right with you if I examined you? I want to check on your baby."

Andi consented, and with less embarrassment and discomfort than she would have thought possible, the doctor made a thorough examination. When she was dressed and seated upright once more, he gave her a reassuring smile. "Everything looks good," he said. "You are not yet in labor, though you are effaced two centimeters."

Her face must have betrayed her confusion, because he added, "Your body is preparing for the upcoming delivery. The baby is shifting into position for birth and your cervix is getting thinner."

"How long before the baby is born?" she asked.

"I take it this is your first child?"

She nodded.

"It could be a couple of weeks or a few days."

"What was the pain?" she asked.

He glanced around the room, at the overturned tables and broken glass, at Simon standing by the window, his back to them. "The person who telephoned me said there had been an altercation. I assume the person who did this—" He nodded to indicate the mess "—is gone now?"

"Yes," she said. Daniel was gone, though she wondered if Simon was right, and he would return.

"The pain was probably a stress reaction. A particularly sharp kick, a tension in the muscles." The doctor shrugged. "What matters now is that you don't worry about it, and try to get some rest." He patted her hand. "You are young and strong and everything looks as it should be. When is your due date?"

"I'm not sure," she said.

He raised one eyebrow, but didn't comment, merely stood there. Simon turned toward them. "How is she?" he asked, though Andi was certain he had been eavesdropping on their conversation.

"She is fine," the doctor said. "All she needs is rest and no stress."

"Would you mind waiting with her here for a few minutes?" Simon asked.

"For a few moments," the doctor agreed.

Simon left the room. The doctor looked down at Andi once more. "This cop—he is a friend of yours?"

"Not exactly," she said. She was sure the doctor was curious, but she refused to elaborate—not that she could have found words to explain the bizarre situation in which she had suddenly found herself.

Simon returned in less than five minutes, carrying a black backpack. "Thank you," he said to the doctor. "You can go now."

As soon as the door shut behind the doctor, Andi sat up. "What happened to the Prophet?" she asked.

"He got away," Simon said. "But the Denver police are looking for him. And hotel security will be watching for him."

"When you find him, promise you won't hurt him," she said.

He glared at her. "He didn't have any problem hurting you."

She flinched at the anger in his voice. "He's terrified. He's never been in a situation like this before," she said. "I'm sure when he calms down he'll cooperate."

"Save your breath," Simon said. "No matter how much you want to believe it, Daniel Metwater isn't the saint he's been pretending to be. My guess is this isn't his first run-in with the law."

Was Simon right? How much did she know about the Prophet, really? But he had always been so gentle and kind to her. She couldn't make the crazed, angry man who had confronted her tonight fit with her previous experience with him. "What are you doing?" she asked as Simon set the backpack on the floor at the end of the sofa.

"I'm staying here tonight."

"You can't do that."

"I can and I will."

"I don't want you here," she protested.

"Maybe not, but you need me."

She swallowed down the fear his words kindled in her. "He left," she said. "He won't come back."

"You don't really believe that, do you?" He sat on the sofa, only a few inches from her feet. "He won't give up that easily, and when he returns, you'll be glad I'm here. What did he say to you while he was here?"

"He wanted my help to get out of here. He planned to dress up in some of my clothes and pretend to be my sister."

"Did you refuse to help him? Is that what set him off?"

She put a hand to her cheek, remembering the sting of the slap. "I asked him about Michelle and Hunter. I asked if it was true that he tried to hurt them. He became very angry and slapped me. Why would he do that? He's never done anything like that before."

"He knows we're closing in on him," Simon said. "I think he's trying to destroy everyone who could provide evidence against him."

"But what do I know that could possibly hurt him?" she asked.

Simon regarded her coolly. "You've lived with him how long now? About six months?"

"Five."

"You're closer to him than anyone else."

They were the same words Michelle had used. But they weren't true. "He isn't really close to anyone."

Simon angled toward her, one arm along the back of the sofa. Weariness pulled at his eyes, and the dark shadow of beard showed along his jaw. If he had driven from Montrose this morning, that meant he had been up for hours. "Help me understand," he said. "What is it about Metwater that attracted you? Why leave everything to live in the middle of nowhere with him? Seems to me you had it pretty good before you hooked up with him."

"That's because people like you think money solves everything," she said. "My life was shallow and meaningless before I met the Prophet and heard him talk about what really matters."

"And what is that?" he asked.

"Living in community. Being close to nature. Focusing on things of real worth, not merely those of monetary value."

She braced herself, prepared for him to mock her, but he only nodded his head thoughtfully. "Those things are certainly important," he said. "The problem with Metwater's approach is that his idea of community is to live apart and isolated. He didn't contribute to society, he only took from it. He liked to pass himself off as a giver, but really, he's just a user. He used you."

She hugged her arms across her chest and glared at him. "You're one to talk," she said. "You don't care about me. You only want evidence for your case."

His expression hardened. "You're right. I want to build a case that will put Daniel Metwater away for years. He's the worst kind of criminal—he pretends to care about people, then he takes advantage of the most vulnerable."

"You're wrong! You haven't seen how he's helped so many people. He's helped addicts quit drugs and ex-convicts go straight."

"Yeah? At what price? He takes everything they have and makes them believe they need him to survive."

"Maybe they do," she said. "Not everyone is capable of living in normal society."

"Then that's sadder still," he said.

She turned away from him, not wanting him to read the confusion and hurt in her eyes. She wasn't an idiot. She recognized that some of what he said was true. But why couldn't he see that the good Daniel had done outweighed the bad? Yes, he had struck her, but that was only one more sign of how afraid and desperate he was. She couldn't wrap her mind around the idea that he was a violent man.

Simon stood. "Try to get some sleep," he said. "Tomorrow, we're headed back to Montrose."

"You can go," she said. "I'm staying here."

"You don't have a say in the matter," Simon said. "As of now, you're officially in protective custody."

Chapter Four

Simon shifted on the hotel suite sofa, unable to get comfortable. Not that he was expecting to sleep—he had his gun on the coffee table within easy reach, ready in case Daniel Metwater returned. Though the local police and hotel security were looking for the Prophet, Simon didn't have confidence that they would find him. The two patrolmen who had responded to the hotel security call earlier had treated the incident as a domestic dispute between a woman and her boyfriend. They hadn't taken Simon's assertion that Daniel Metwater was a dangerous fugitive seriously.

But Simon knew better. Now that Michelle Munson—Starfall—and her child were out of his reach in a safe house elsewhere in the state, Metwater was focused on Andi Matheson. He only had to get hold of her and keep her alive two more days, until her twenty-fifth birthday, and he would have everything he wanted— her money and her permanent silence after he killed her.

Simon had stretched the truth a little when he told Andi she was in protective custody. He couldn't force her to accept his protection, but it was the only way he could think of to make sure she was safe.

She refused to see the danger. Even after he had struck her, she still thought of Daniel Metwater as a prophet who only wanted to do good. Metwater had spent a lot of money cultivating that image, but Simon knew scum when he saw it. His line of work put him on a first-name basis with the worst of the worst—coyotes who took every dime a poor laborer ever made, then abandoned him and his family to die in the desert far from home. Men who promised to protect a young girl and find her a good job across the border, only to sell her into slavery in an illegal brothel in the city. Metwater was no better than those kind of abusers. He had managed to make Andi believe the best she deserved from him was to be one of many women he slept with, privileged to work as his unpaid secretary and be at his beck and call.

Maybe the other men in her life—her father and the man who was the father of her unborn child—had made her think she didn't deserve to be treated better. They were both dead now, and as far as Simon could determine, no great loss there.

If he had a woman like Andi in his life, he would treat her with the care she deserved. He would make her his partner, not his servant, and protect her with his own life, if necessary.

Not that he'd ever have anyone like Andi. She was used to men with money and power and sophistication. Simon had none of those things. He was a hard man who spent his life doing hard, sometimes ugly things. Somebody had to do the things he did, but Andi deserved better. She deserved someone as good as she was.

He sighed and closed his eyes once more, willing himself to rest. He had done everything he knew to protect her. He had done what he could to make it tougher for Metwater to get to Andi.

But not impossible. That small room for doubt was what made every cop's job a walk along a razor's edge. There was always some aspect of the situation he couldn't see, some action he couldn't plan for.

The phone at his belt vibrated. He withdrew it and frowned at the unfamiliar number. "Hello?" he answered, speaking softly so as not to wake Andi in the next room.

"Officer Woolridge? This is Owen Pogue—one of the security guards here at the hotel."

Simon sat up. "Yes? What is it?"

"This might not be connected to the man you're looking for, but one of the housekeeping staff was assaulted on the third floor about half an hour ago. Whoever did it came up behind her, threw a blanket over her and shoved her into one of the supply closets. He didn't really hurt her, but he took her keys."

Simon was on his feet, headed for the door. "Did she get a look at the man?"

"No, sir. He surprised her. Do you think it's your guy?"

"It could be. You still have the photo I sent you?"

"Yes, sir. I shared it with everyone on staff—

not many people this time of night. The housekeeper was the only one on duty in her department."

"Did you call the police?"

Pogue hesitated. "Did you?" Simon demanded.

"I let them know we had had an incident. But management doesn't like a police presence here. It upsets the guests. I told them we had everything under control."

Simon ground his teeth together, holding back a flood of curses. "Put someone at every exit, watching for him," he said.

"Sir, I only have three people in my department tonight, and the hotel has half a dozen entrances."

Simon didn't even waste his breath swearing. "Do the best you can," he said. "He may have already left, but the fact that he has a set of keys makes me think not. He's probably hiding somewhere in the hotel. It would be better if we could search the rooms."

"We could never do that without a warrant," Pogue said. "Management would fight it, for sure. The guests would throw a fit, especially since, at this time of night, it would mean getting most of them out of bed."

Simon knew Pogue was right. He was an out-of-town cop chasing a man wanted for out-of-town crimes. No Denver judge was going to agree to kick a bunch of wealthy, and in some cases famous, people out of their posh hotel rooms in the middle of the night for a random search. Bottom line—Simon was pretty much on his own with this one. "Let me know if anything else happens that doesn't feel right to you," he said, and ended the call.

He walked to the bedroom and tried the door. Not locked. Was it because Andi didn't see him as a threat? More likely, she had been too exhausted and upset to think of setting the lock.

She had made a mound of blankets on one side of the king-size bed, illuminated by the glow of the digital clock. Simon stood in the doorway for a long moment, watching the gentle rise and fall of her body, listening to the soft sigh of her breathing. The room smelled of her perfume—something floral and expensive, and a luxury she apparently hadn't given up when she had moved to the wilderness. He had smelled it before, on his visits to camp.

After assuring himself she was sleeping well, he slipped across the room to the door that connected this suite with the one next to it, allowing the two apartments to be opened into one larger unit. He verified that the deadbolt was turned and the safety chain in place. Even if Metwater had a master key that would allow him to get into the room next door, he wouldn't be able to come through here.

He was moving back toward the door when the woman in the bed stirred. "What are you doing?" she asked, her voice clear and calm— not the voice of someone who had just awakened.

"I was checking the door lock."

"Why?"

He hesitated. No sense explaining about the maid and the missing keys and his suspicion that Metwater was still in the hotel. Why frighten her? "I'm obsessive about locks," he said instead.

"You would be," she said, and rolled over, her back to him.

The retort almost made him smile. He liked that she didn't take him too seriously. He returned to his place on the sofa and lay back down, eyes open, waiting.

ANDI SHIFTED POSITION in the big, overly soft bed for the dozenth time, her mind as restless as her body. She had slept only briefly, awakening to the feel of someone watching her. She had realized right away it was Simon. The tall, edgy cop didn't frighten her, though his refusal to see any good in the Prophet frustrated her, and the accusations he made against a man she loved confused her.

His words stuck in her head—what he had said about Daniel stealing not only people's possessions, but their independence. To someone like Simon, autonomy probably seemed like something valuable, but Andi wasn't so sure.

She had never really been on her own. As her father's daughter, she had been protected and watched over, scrutinized even, by photographers and gossip columnists and hangers-on who coveted her beauty or her money or her power—none of which she could claim any control over. The beauty was a trick of genetics she had been born with, and the money and power belonged to her father, not her. She had been pampered and educated, groomed for a life as the wife of another rich man or politician like her father. She had never questioned her upbringing or desired a particular career. She had accepted everything she received as her due.

And then she had discovered she was going to have a baby, and something inside of her shifted. She had glimpsed a different kind of future, one as wife to the man she loved, mother to a little girl or boy. But the man she had given herself to hadn't loved her—not really. He already had a wife and family. Discovering that had shocked all the love out of her—though maybe her feelings hadn't really been love, but instead the self-deception of someone who wanted so badly to be valued for herself and not merely for her looks or her name or her money.

The Prophet had promised to give her that value. He told her she was special—and he had made her feel special. He didn't flatter her beauty or measure her wealth or talk about her power. He simply looked into her eyes and told her he loved her.

And she had believed him. Now this cop was telling her different, and she wanted to deny his lies. Except something deep inside her told her that maybe he wasn't lying. That maybe she was the one deceiving herself.

Her cell phone buzzed, and she fished it out from under the pillow and answered it. "Hello?" she whispered.

"Are you all right, Asteria?" The Prophet's voice was soothing, full of concern, addressing her by the name he had given her—a name for a goddess, he had said. Her heart beat faster at the sound of it.

"I'm worried about you," she said.

"I'll be all right," he said. "Good is stronger than evil. Haven't I always told you that?"

"Yes." But what was evil? Was Simon evil? She couldn't see it.

"I need you to help me," the Prophet said.

"Yes. Of course."

"I know that cop is watching you, but you don't need to be afraid of him."

"I'm not afraid." She had never been afraid of Simon, though she couldn't say why.

"Because you're good, and your goodness makes you strong," Daniel said.

She waited, not sure how to answer this.

"I need you to do one small thing for me," he said. "But don't let the cop see."

"All right."

"Go to the door that connects your bedroom

to the one next door, and open the deadlock and slide back the chain."

She looked toward the door, the one Simon had checked.

"Can you do that?" Metwater asked.

"Yes. But why?"

"Don't worry about the why. 'Only obey and all good will come to you.'" The words were from a chant he had taught them. One she always found especially calming.

"Only obey, and all good will come to me," she repeated.

"That's right."

"What do I do after I open the locks?" she asked.

"Wait."

He ended the call, and she slid the phone back under her pillow. Then, listening for any movement from the seating area, she tiptoed to the connecting door and carefully turned the knob for the deadbolt, then slid back the chain. It rattled against the doorframe and she froze, heart pounding, not daring to breathe. But she heard nothing from the other room.

She went to the bathroom, then returned to the bed to wait.

She didn't have to wait long. She felt rather than heard a shift in the air as the door connecting her suite to the one next door eased open. A shadow filled the doorway, and then Daniel was beside her, kneeling on the bed, his lips brushing hers with a soft kiss. She reached up to put her arms around him, but he gently pushed her away.

He put his lips against her ear and spoke so softly that she had to strain to make out the words. "I couldn't leave without you," he said. "I risked everything to come back and be with you. Do you understand?"

"Yes." The answer was automatic, but not

exactly truthful. Why would he risk capture to be with her? "It's too dangerous for you here," she whispered.

"Not with you by my side. You'll protect me." He brought his hand up to caress her shoulder, then moved toward her breast, going still when his fingers brushed the locket pendant. "What is this?" he asked, pulling it from beneath her gown, the chain tightening around her throat.

"It…it's the necklace you told me you would give my baby," she said. "I know I shouldn't have taken it without permission, but I wanted it to help me feel close to you while we were so far apart."

She braced herself against his anger, but instead, he kissed her cheek. "Bless you," he said. "I knew you were my good luck charm." He reached for her hand and she shied away, remembering when he had struck her not an hour before.

"It's all right," he said soothingly. "I would never let any harm come to you."

This time she let him take her hand. As much as experience told her not to trust him, her memories of how good things had once been between them beguiled her into cooperating.

"Come on," he urged. "We have to hurry."

"Where are we going?" she asked.

"A safe place. I promise."

The bed creaked as she shoved herself into a sitting position on the side, and stretched out her feet to find her shoes.

Metwater pulled her roughly up while she was still searching, and she made an involuntary cry of protest.

The bedroom door opened, spilling light into the room. Simon stood in the doorway. "Andi, are you all right?" he asked.

Before she could answer, Metwater clapped his hand over her mouth and pulled her tight against him. Something stung her throat and she gave another cry. Light flooded the room, and Metwater's voice filled the silence. "Drop the gun, or I swear I'll cut her throat and she'll bleed to death right here."

Chapter Five

Time slowed, every sense magnified as the two men faced off. The blade of the knife glinted in the glow of the crystal chandelier overhead. A single crimson jewel of blood slid down Andi's pale neck. Simon focused on the strong beat of her pulse at the base of her throat, and his own heart matched its rhythm.

"Drop your gun," Metwater ordered.

Simon crouched and laid the weapon on the carpet, Andi's gaze fixed on him.

"The other one, too," Metwater said. "In the ankle holster."

Simon complied, then straightened. He glanced toward the connecting door, which stood partially open. He should have stationed Pogue or one of his men there.

"What are you looking at?" Metwater shifted and Andi gasped, a fresh bead of blood forming.

Simon looked into Metwater's eyes. Gone was the handsome, arrogant man so assured of getting away with whatever he wanted. He didn't have an army of followers and lawyers protecting him now. It was only him against Simon. Metwater had the woman and the knife, which he thought gave him the advantage.

Simon shifted his gaze back to the door. "Pogue, now!" he shouted, and dropped to the floor.

Metwater jerked toward the door. Andi's scream bounced off the walls in the small room as Simon scooped up his Glock and fired. But in trying to make sure he didn't hit the woman, he caught Metwater in the shoulder.

Not a killing shot. But enough to make him drop the knife. Simon aimed again as Metwater lurched from the bed toward the door.

Andi's screams changed pitch, interspersed with sobbing. "I'm bleeding to death!"

If Simon pursued Metwater, he could probably catch him, but at what cost?

He moved toward the bed, where Andi sat, clutching her throat, the sheets and her gown stained crimson. He pulled out his phone and dialed 911 as he crossed the room. He identified himself and explained the situation as succinctly as possible.

"Yes, sir. I'm dispatching an ambulance. Please stay on the line."

But he had already hung up and pocketed the phone. Andi stared at him, eyes huge in her pale face, hands clutched to her throat. She was still conscious—that was a good sign. "Let me take a look," Simon said. He took both her hands in his and gently tugged them toward her lap.

She resisted. "It's all right," he said. "I promise I won't hurt you."

She lowered her hands, and he studied the two six-inch long slashes where blood was already beginning to clot. Relief flooded him. "The cuts are shallow," he said. "You'll be sore, but you shouldn't even have a scar once they heal."

"But there's so much blood." She looked down at her hands.

"You have a lot of blood vessels in your head and neck," he said. "But he didn't sever any arteries. The ambulance is on its way to check you over and make sure everything is okay."

Tears welled in her eyes. "He tried to kill me," she said. "Why?"

He could go over the old arguments about why Metwater wanted her dead, but now wasn't the time. "I won't let him hurt you again," he said.

"Where is he now?"

"He ran. But he won't get far."

"You shot him." He couldn't tell if the idea frightened or comforted her.

"I did. That will slow him down. He'll have to get help, and when he does, we'll bring him in."

He had already gotten through to a supervisor at the Denver Police Department. He hoped this second attack would shock them into real action. They were sending over a senior officer, and soon every cop in the city would be looking for the man who had tried to kill a young woman at the Brown Palace. Simon would try to keep Andi's name out of the news, but the information was bound to leak eventually.

Andi Matheson had been one of the beautiful people who had been a fixture at every prominent social function in Denver and DC. Her disappearance five months ago, and subsequent reports that she had become Daniel Metwater's most devoted follower, had kept the interest in her alive. News that she had resurfaced—and that she had been almost killed by the man she had given up pretty much everything for—would be enough to send the media into a frenzy.

He pulled out his phone and called Pogue. "An ambulance and the Denver Police are on their way over," he said. "Direct them to Ms. Daniels's suite."

"Is she okay? What happened?"

"Metwater came back. She's frightened, but she'll be okay."

"Where is he now?"

"I don't know. But he's wounded and he's got a knife."

"I'll let my men know."

The room phone rang, the bell loud and jarring. Simon answered it. "Ms. Daniels?" The woman on the other end sounded unsure.

"This is Officer Woolridge. I'm with Ms. Daniels."

"This is Cami at the front desk. There's an ambulance here, and two police officers."

"Send them up."

Five minutes later, the room was full of people—three EMTs, two police officers, Pogue and another man who said he was with hotel management. Simon started to move away from the bed, but Andi grabbed his hand. "Don't leave me!" she pleaded.

"I won't go far," he said. "But I need to let the EMTs examine you."

One of the emergency medical technicians moved in alongside Simon. "It'll be all right, ma'am," he said. "You'll feel a lot better once we get this checked out and cleaned up."

Simon stepped back, and a wiry black man in uniform tapped him on the shoulder. "You Simon Woolridge?" he asked.

"I'm with Immigration and Customs Enforcement." Simon showed his badge.

"Sergeant Tyson Daley." Sergeant Daley glanced at the bed, where two EMTs were bent over Andi. "She an illegal?"

"I'm on special assignment with the Ranger Brigade, working out of Black Canyon of the Gunnison National Park. We're a federal task force focused on crime on public lands."

"You're a few hundred miles out of your territory, aren't you?" Daley asked.

"I came to Denver to apprehend a fugitive,

Daniel Metwater," Simon said. "He's the one who cut her."

"We had a report of a domestic dispute here earlier," Daley said. "This the same guy?"

"It is. He must have hidden in the hotel until he saw his chance to get at her again."

"Tell me what happened," Daley said.

"I shot him—got him in the shoulder, I think."

Daley didn't look happy about this news. "So now we're looking for a wounded crazy guy with a knife. What do you want him for, anyway?"

"Kidnapping and attempted murder, for starters. But he may be connected to several other crimes."

Daley pulled out a tablet computer. "Okay. Let me get some particulars and we'll put out an APB and alert the local hospitals and emergency clinics. I'm gonna need a statement from you and from Ms. Daniels."

Simon didn't bother telling him he would have to wait for his statement. As soon as Simon was satisfied that Andi was safe, he was going to follow Metwater's trail himself. While he wouldn't be upset if the locals caught up with the Prophet before he hurt anyone else, Simon wanted the satisfaction of being the one to track him down.

He gave Daley the information he needed, then excused himself. "I need to call in to my commander," he said.

Though it was after two in the morning, Commander Graham Ellison of the Ranger Brigade answered on the fourth ring. "Ellison."

"It's Simon. I'm here with Andi Matheson at the Brown Palace in Denver. Metwater tried to get to her. I wounded him, but he got away."

"I'm listening." Simon pictured the commander moving from his bedroom to his home office, transitioning from family man to cop. "Tell me everything."

Simon summed up all that had happened since he had arrived in Denver. "I'm going after Metwater," he concluded. "But first I need to make sure Andi is safe."

"Do you think she's still a target?" Graham asked.

"Yes," Simon said. "He's going to come back for her."

"Then stay with her," the commander ordered. "Be ready when he comes back."

"Yes, sir."

"We obtained a warrant and searched his motor home," the commander said. "The team is still sorting through everything we found— a number of items that apparently belonged to his brother, as well as items from the family business in Chicago."

"Anything that links him directly to a crime?" Simon asked. He wanted everything they could find to throw at Metwater in court, so that he would stay behind bars for a very long time.

"Not yet," Ellison said. "Michelle Munson says he has a necklace that belonged to her sister—the one she thinks David Metwater murdered—but we haven't located it. We're still looking though."

"What about the rest of his followers?"

"A few are still in camp, but most of them have moved out—back to family or old hangouts. We have a census and asked them to provide contact information. A couple had outstanding warrants, and we turned them over to the Montrose sheriff's office."

"Any clue where Metwater would go to hide?" Simon asked. "Any other property he owns? Friends? Relatives?"

"We haven't found anything like that yet, but we're looking. I'll keep you posted."

"Something else you could look into for me," Simon said. "There's a Russian guy, midthirties, blond with a goatee. He approached Andi in the hotel lobby last night—called her by her real name and pretended they had met at some social function a while back. She swears she had never seen him before. He was asking about Metwater."

"If he's Russian, he won't be a friend of Metwater's," the commander said.

"That's what I'm thinking."

"I'll see what we can find out about him."

Simon ended the call, and one of the EMTs approached. "The wounds aren't severe, but she's had quite a shock," the tech said. "With her advanced pregnancy, we'd like to take her in to the hospital to be monitored overnight."

Simon glanced over the man's shoulder and

found Andi's gaze fixed on him. "What does she think of the idea?"

"She doesn't want to go, but she's worried about the baby. She said she would consent if it was all right with you."

"Tell her I'll come with her."

"That would be great."

"Tell her I won't leave her." Not until he knew she was safe. Metwater wouldn't give up yet. Andi Matheson wasn't the kind of woman a man left behind.

VICTOR KRAYEV SAT in his rental car across the street from the Brown Palace Hotel, cell phone clamped to his ear. "I had to leave the hotel," he said. "There's a cop in there who's watching Andi Matheson. He started questioning me, and I figured I'd better lay low for a while."

"Why is he watching her?" the man on the other end of the line asked. He was the one who had hired Victor for this job, and for many others.

"Maybe the same reason I'm here—he wants Metwater."

"He can wait in line."

"When we get through with Metwater, there won't be anything left for the police," Victor said.

"Did you talk to the woman?"

"I approached her in the lobby. I pretended we had met before, at a party. She seemed upset that I knew her real name—she's registered at the hotel under an alias—Daniels."

"Metwater probably thought of that. He believes he's so clever."

"I asked her about Metwater, but the cop interfered before she could answer. I'm sure she's in contact with him though. Metwater made the reservation at the hotel and personally delivered her here. And she's going to have his kid any day now. Not to mention she's loaded. If he's planning on skipping town, my bet is he's going to take her with him."

"Do whatever it takes to get him. And the key. We must have that key."

"I know my job. I haven't failed you yet, have I?"

"Don't let this be the first time."

He ended the call and tucked the phone back inside his jacket. The lights from the hotel cast a golden glow over the warm brown stone of the facade, though many of the rooms were dark and only a few people came and went from the lobby. Daniel Metwater wasn't one of them.

Flashing lights distracted him, and he turned to see an ambulance approaching. It pulled up to the hotel, followed by two Denver Police cars. Victor sat forward, straining for a better look.

Then he dug out his phone and dialed the hotel number. "Welcome to the Brown Palace Hotel and Spa. This is Cami. How may I—"

"Cami, it's Vince. How are you doing, beautiful?"

"Oh, Vince. Hi." Her voice took on a girlish flutter. "I'm good. How are you?"

"I'm good, gorgeous. I just drove by on my way downtown and saw the cop cars and an ambulance. What's going on over there?"

"Oh, um, well. I'm not sure I'm supposed to say."

"Aw come on. Who am I gonna tell? I just want to know if it's safe to come back and see you again."

"Oh, I'm sure it's safe." She lowered her voice. "I had to move away from the desk. I guess the cops are here because there was a fight upstairs. It happens sometimes. Word is some woman got cut."

"What woman? Do you know her name?"

"I'm sure I'm not supposed to say that." Her tone was teasing. Flirtatious.

He mirrored it. "How about if I guess and you tell me if I'm right?" he asked. "Was it Ms. Daniels, up on the fourteenth floor?"

She gasped. "How did you know?"

He hadn't known. But since Andi Matheson was the only occupant of the hotel he cared about, hers was the only name he had to throw out there. "Lucky guess," he said. "Is she going to be all right? Do they know who cut her?"

"I don't know who did it, but I guess he got away, because I overheard security talking with one of the cops about looking for him. But I don't know any more than that. Honestly, I don't."

"There's another man there," Victor said. "A plainclothes cop. Dark hair and eyes. He's wearing jeans and a black shirt. What's his name?"

"Do you mean Mr. Woolridge? He has the room two doors down from Ms. Daniels. Is he really a cop?"

"That's him," Victor said. "I thought I recognized him—an old friend I haven't seen in a long while. I'll have to say hello to him next time I'm at the hotel."

"When will that be?" Cami asked. "When will I see you again?"

He cringed at the whine in her voice. "Soon," he said. "You don't think I could stay away from you long, do you?"

She giggled. "I have to go now," she said. "Call me back in an hour or two, after the commotion has died down."

"Sure thing, darling." He ended the call. Cami wouldn't be hearing from Vince again, but she didn't have to know that. Victor would

keep an eye on the ambulance, and on its occupant. He would bet gold that Daniel Metwater was the one who had cut Andi. Maybe
she had given him grief about the trouble he
was in, or she didn't want to leave her cushy
hotel. He had cut her, but something or someone had interrupted him—the cop Victor had
met in the bar?

Maybe, but Metwater wasn't one to leave a
job unfinished. He would be back. And when
he showed up, Victor would be there. The
man owed a debt, and Victor fully intended
to collect.

Chapter Six

Andi woke to soft pink light reflected off walls the color of clouds at sunset. Lime-sherbet tinted sheets covered her, and the gentle beeping of a monitor and low murmur of distant voices provided soothing background sounds that threatened to lull her back to sleep. Then she swallowed, and the ache at her throat reminded her of everything that had happened last night. Heart pounding, she looked around and spotted Simon, slumped in a chair beside the bed, asleep.

He needed a shave, as evidenced by the suggestion of a dark beard along his jaw, and his shirt was rumpled, his hair uncombed. He looked dangerous, but seeing him there calmed her. As she studied him, he stirred and opened his eyes. "How are you feeling?" he asked, his voice rough from sleep.

"A little sore, but okay." Better than she would have expected. She smoothed the sheets over her belly. "The doctors said everything checked out okay. I guess I was lucky."

He made a noise she took for assent, and stretched.

"What time is it?" she asked, looking for, but not finding, a clock.

"Morning."

"Have you been here all night?" The thought touched her.

"I didn't want to leave you."

"What happened to the Prophet?" she asked. "Did you find him?"

"Not yet. But every cop in the state is looking for him. He won't get away."

"I won't be safe until you capture him." Saying the words made her feel heavy with sadness.

"No. But we will capture him."

She looked away, trying to process this thought. It was what she wanted—Daniel Metwater locked away so he could never hurt her again. But she had a hard time reconciling the man who had hurt her—the one she was so afraid of now—with the man she had followed and adored for the past seven months.

She slid her hand up to clutch the necklace. Daniel hadn't minded that she had taken it. Was that because it was evidence he had been involved in a crime, and now that she had it, he thought the police couldn't link it to him? Michelle had talked about a necklace that belonged to her sister, who had died of an overdose in David Metwater's apartment. But maybe the sister had given it to David, and that was why Daniel, as his brother's heir, had it.

Andi shook her head. It was all so confusing.

The door to the room opened and a slender man in green scrubs hurried in. "Ms. Daniels, how are you feeling this morning?" he asked. "I'm Dr. Ogilvie. I saw you last night."

"I'm fine," she said. "Very well, thank you."

Dr. Ogilvie studied the array of machines and nodded, apparently satisfied. "As I said last night, keeping you for observation was just a precaution. No worries. As soon as I sign the discharge papers, you're free to go, though you'll want to take it easy and avoid stress." He looked at Simon when he spoke the last words.

"I'll take care of her," Simon said.

The doctor opened his mouth as if to say more, but his gaze shifted to the gun at Simon's side and he pressed his lips together, silent.

The doctor was scarcely out the door when a nurse bustled in, long braids gathered in a ponytail atop her head. "I'm here to unhook you from all the monitors and help you get dressed," she said. She scowled at Simon. "You can go get coffee down the hall while we're busy. You look as if you need it."

As Simon left the room, Andi resisted the urge to call after him. She had never been one to startle at shadows before, so she wasn't going to start now.

"He wouldn't budge from your side all night," the nurse said as she began disconnecting tubes and switching off machines. "Sat in that chair all night and glared at anyone who came near you. I've seen overprotective husbands before, but he beats them all. Must be the cop thing."

Andi let the words flow over her, not bothering to correct the woman's assumption that Simon was her husband. If she had had someone to protect her so fiercely all along, maybe she wouldn't be in such a fix now.

The nurse pressed a bandage over the small hole where the IV needle had been inserted. "All untethered now," she said. "Your clothes are in the little cabinet in the bathroom. You can shower if you like. Do you need any help?"

"No, thank you."

"There's a call button in the bathroom if you need anything, or your husband can always help you."

She hurried away, and Andi shuffled to the bathroom, the idea of Simon helping her undress—and shower—sending a not-unpleasant flutter of arousal through her. Where had that come from?

By the time she emerged from the bathroom twenty minutes later, freshly showered and wearing the slacks, top and boots that Simon or someone must have fetched from her hotel room, she felt much more alert and ready to face whatever lay ahead.

Simon was sitting in the chair by her bed. He handed her a cup of coffee. "If you don't drink coffee, or you're not supposed to have it, I can get something else," he said. "Tea or milk or juice."

"Coffee's good." She sipped from the cup. The coffee was heavily laced with cream and sugar—just the way she liked it. She had tried to limit her caffeine during her pregnancy, but she couldn't give it up altogether.

Simon looked around the room. "Do you have anything to take with you?"

The gown she had arrived in had been stained with blood—she shuddered at the memory. In any case, it had been discarded and quickly ex-changed for a hospital smock. She shook her head. "No. What will we do now?"

"We'll go back to the hotel for the rest of your things," he said. "But then we need to leave." He opened a closet and pulled out a full-length faux-mink coat. "Put this on. It's cold out. Weather forecasters are predicting snow."

The Prophet had given her that coat. It screamed expense and privilege, and now it made her skin crawl to wear it.

"Come on." Simon held it out. "You need to stay warm."

She swallowed hard and nodded. He was right, and it was just a coat. *Things don't matter*, the Prophet had preached. She had believed him, even when his actions contradicted the words. He wore expensive designer clothing and insisted on the best accommodations when he traveled, even when some of his followers lived in patched-together tents and trailers. How was it the contradictions hadn't bothered her before?

She put on the coat and walked beside Simon to the elevator. "I don't see how you walk in those heels," he said, looking down at her stiletto boots. "But they were the only shoes I could find to bring up here."

"I'm used to them," she said. "And they're the only shoes I brought with me. I really didn't think I would be staying in Denver that long."

They stopped in front of the elevator and he hit the down button. "Where are we going now?" she asked.

"I'm taking you back to Montrose, to a safe house."

She started to protest that she wanted to go home, but it wasn't as if she could go back to the Family's camp—if there was even a camp left. Her father was in prison and her baby's father was dead. She had no close relatives. She had the money and resources to live on her own, but not the will—at least not right now.

"Is the rest of the Family still in our camp?" she asked.

"A few. Without Metwater there, most of them have gone back to their families, or to their old lives."

"He was what held us together," she said.

"Doesn't say much for a belief system if it all depends on one man, does it?" he said.

She glared at him. "Whatever you think of the man—whatever he is now—he did a lot of good," she said. "I won't stop believing that."

"If that makes you happy, I'm not going to stop you," he said. "But as far as I can tell, nothing he said was original. He was just good at plagiarizing."

"Are you always so cynical?" she asked.

"Yes."

"You don't believe there's good in the world?"

"There's good," he said. "But the real saints in this world do good things instead of merely talking about them." He took her arm. "Let's go. I want to get on the road before the traffic gets heavy."

Someone had cleaned her room at the Brown Palace, removing the broken glass and blood-ied sheets, polishing the furniture and fresh-ening the flowers, even replacing the broken lamp with one that looked identical. "Pack what you'll need for a few nights in one bag," Simon said as he crossed the room to look out the window at the downtown scene below. "Anything else we'll ask the front desk to send on to Montrose."

"I only brought one bag with me." At his sur-prised look, she laughed. "I'm not a spoiled socialite anymore," she said. "If nothing else, the Prophet taught me to travel light."

"There's something else you've learned since being with him," Simon said, his expression serious once more. "Something he doesn't want you to tell the rest of the world. If we can figure out what that is, it could be the key to stopping him."

"If I knew, I promise I would tell you," she said. "But until he turned against me, I never knew anything bad about him."

"Keep thinking," Simon said. "You know something, and I'd like to find out what it is before he tries to kill you again."

She froze, one hand on the doorknob to the bedroom. "He's on the run," she said. "He knows you're looking for him. He won't risk trying to get at me again."

"A smart man wouldn't do that, no. But a desperate man would. And from what I've seen, Daniel Metwater is a very desperate man."

"Are you trying to frighten me?" she asked.

"I'm being honest with you. Would you rather I told you pretty lies?"

His eyes met hers, and the steadiness of his gaze made her feel less shaky. "No," she said. "I've been lied to enough in my life." Maybe an honest man—even one who didn't spare her feelings—was worth sticking with, at least for a while.

By the time they left the hotel, low clouds had blanketed the area, blotting out the sun. The air had the cold, heavy feeling of imminent snow. At least Andi wouldn't have to worry about keeping warm in that coat of hers. Simon pulled his sheepskin-lined jacket out of the back of his cruiser, along with leather gloves, ready for whatever the weather brought.

Andi wasn't a chatterbox, that was for sure, which was fine by Simon. He had a reputation as not much of a talker himself. He preferred action to words, most of the time anyway. He glanced over at his passenger as they waited at a red light, trying to gauge her mood. Not nervous or afraid. He would have said she was calm, even.

So far, he had been pretty impressed with her, something he hadn't expected. She looked delicate and weak, but when push came to shove, she had nerves of steel. She had been threatened, cut, examined by strangers and betrayed by her lover, yet she hadn't wilted or whined or complained. She was struggling with her emotions—he hadn't missed the moments of troubled silence or brief tears—but she was keeping it together.

The light changed and he turned right onto a side street, drove two blocks, then made another right. "What are you doing?" Andi asked.

He made another right. "I'm driving," he said.

"That's the second time we've passed that car wash," she said, nodding to the Sudzy Ride sign.

"I'm making sure we aren't being followed. Nice to know you're paying attention."

"I'm not as dumb as I look."

"I never thought you were dumb." Naive, misled and too trusting, but not dumb.

"Then you don't believe the stereotype?"

He headed up the entrance ramp to Interstate 70. "And what is the stereotype?"

"That blondes are dumb. That beautiful women aren't serious or smart. That rich women only care about shopping." She waved her hand. "I'm familiar with all the assumptions."

"Did you try to prove them wrong?" he asked.

"I studied botany at Brown," she said. "My father told everyone I was learning to grow roses and arrange flowers. He thought it was more suitable than telling people I was interested in science."

"What century was he living in again?"

"Oh, he was positively Victorian. But he wasn't alone. Plenty of rich men want wives who look good, do good and keep their mouths shut. He couldn't imagine why I wasn't excited about the prospect."

"Is your mother that type?" he asked.

"She wasn't. But she married my father before he had money. And she died when I was fifteen."

"I lost mine when I was sixteen," he said. This confession—the intimacy of it—surprised him. He never talked about his family.

"Mine died of cancer," she said. "What happened to yours?"

"She was murdered."

He regretted the words as soon as they were out of his mouth. Andi looked stricken. "How horrible!"

He cleared his throat, as much to buy time to measure his words as to rein in his emotions. "She was a nurse, volunteering at a center for pregnant teens. One of the girls' boyfriends broke into the place, high on drugs. He killed his girlfriend, and then he killed my mom." He still remembered the grayness of the days after that—the darkness of every room, and the hollowness of every conversation, as if the black void left by her absence was taking over the world.

"She sounds like a very good person," Andi said.

"She was."

"And your father?" she asked. "What was he like?"

"He was a cop."

"Like you."

"Not like me. He was a city cop. A street cop. He made a difference in people's lives every day." Simon couldn't say that about his own work. His dad had relationships with the people on his beat. Simon's interactions with both suspects and victims were usually brief.

"Is he still working?"

"He was killed in the line of duty." Set up to take a fall by corrupt bosses he had stood up against, but no sense going into that. An investigation had revealed the truth, and he had been awarded a medal, posthumously. Simon had the medal in a drawer somewhere at home. He couldn't bear to throw it away, but he didn't keep it where he would see it often—a reminder of how the system had failed his father, coming through only when it was too late.

"At least he's someone you can be proud of," Andi said. "Not like my father.'

"Have you had any contact with your father since he went to prison?" Simon asked. Pete Matheson had pleaded guilty to killing Special Agent Frank Asher and was currently serving time in a federal prison near Denver.

"No." Her voice was clipped, and cold enough to send a chill through Simon.

"Has he tried to get in touch with you?"

"I don't know. And I don't care."

But the tears that roughened her words told Simon she did care. He reached out and took her hand. "If you ever do want to see him, I can help arrange that," he said. "And if you don't, that's okay too."

She pulled away from him and wrapped her arm across her belly. "I don't know what I want," she said softly. "Just for all of this to be over. I want to be somewhere quiet, where I can focus on my baby and not think about anything else."

"I'm working on that," he said. "Just hang on a little longer."

She pulled the coat more tightly around her and didn't say anything for a few miles. When sleet began to hit the windows, she turned toward him once more. "I guess winter has fi-nally decided to show up," she said.

The tension in Simon's chest eased at the words. She didn't sound so upset anymore. He wouldn't have blamed her if she had decided to sulk in her misery for a while, but she was stronger than that, and he appreciated it more than he could say. Funny—he wasn't someone who especially liked talking to people, but he was finding that he enjoyed his conversations with her. "It would have been pretty miserable, camped in the woods all winter," he said. "We can get a lot of snow in that country."

"The Prophet talked about heading south for the winter," she said. "Maybe Mexico." She shifted toward him. "Maybe that's where he's gone now. He said he had friends down there." She frowned. "Well, not exactly friends. He said he had 'connections.'"

"I'll mention it to my commander next time

I talk to him," Simon said. "He'll check it out. Is there any place else he mentioned—another house he owned or friends he might turn to for help?"

She shook her head. "None of us talked about our lives before we came to the Family," she said. She had tried a few times to bring up the past, but Daniel had always deflected her attempts to unburden herself, and he had revealed very little of his own history—nothing, she realized now, that hadn't already been written in news stories about him. "The whole point was to start over, with a clean slate. To focus on the present and the future, not the past."

"Kind of makes me wonder what he had in his past that he didn't want to talk about," Simon said.

"Don't tell me you don't have things in your past, things you did or said, that it hurts to remember," she spoke softly. "Choices you made that you wish you could take back."

"Of course I do. Everyone does. But I try to learn from them, not pretend they never happened."

"Not everyone can do that."

"So all that time you spent with him, and he never talked about his past?" Simon asked.

"Not really."

"What about his family?"

"He said his father was a cold man who was only interested in work and money. Greed drove all his decisions and he judged everyone by how much they owned."

"Sounds like he brought his son up to follow in his footsteps," Simon said. "Between his family's wealth and what he was acquiring from his followers, he's put together a considerable fortune." A fortune he couldn't access, since authorities had frozen his accounts.

"Yes, he liked money, but it was never his main focus," she said. "I'm sure of that. If it had been, he would have lived in a mansion, instead of a motor home. With his looks and charisma, he could have been one of those TV evangelists."

"So why didn't he do that?" Simon asked. "Why hide out with a small group of followers in the wilderness?"

"Because he believed that was the way to spiritual purity." She said the words without a hint of sarcasm or irony.

"Or maybe he wanted to keep a low profile because he was afraid of the wrong kind of attention," Simon said. "From what I recall, he was a little paranoid about the Russian mafia."

"Because they killed his brother," Andi said. "David's death affected him deeply."

"David Metwater was suspected of double-crossing his killers," Simon said. "He gambled, did drugs and stole from the family business. He was living the kind of life that pretty much guaranteed he would come to a bad end."

"He was Daniel's twin," Andi said. "His identical twin. It didn't matter that he was living a terrible life. Daniel said they were two halves of a whole. David's death left a void that could never be filled."

"It's a good story," Simon said. "But something tells me there's more to it than that. First, he goes after Michelle Munson—Starfall—because he finds out she's got a scrapbook full of articles about him and his brother. She wants a necklace that belonged to the sister she thought David Metwater murdered. Daniel Metwater would rather kidnap her baby, and try to kill her and a cop, rather than hand over that locket or let us get a good look at that scrapbook. And now he's gone after you."

Andi put a hand to her chest. "When he came

to me last night, he said we were meant to be together."

Simon tightened his grip on the steering wheel. It shouldn't matter, but hearing her sound so lovesick over a man like Metwater caused him physical pain. "Do you believe that?" he asked.

"No." She pulled the coat more tightly around her, though he had turned the heater up to high. "He's not the kind of man who could ever be devoted to one person. I knew that from the first. I told myself it was because he had so many followers to care for, and higher things to focus on."

"Do you still believe that?"

The look on her face was pure misery. "No. I think he's just another man who thinks the world owes him everything."

Simon winced. He was no expert on women, but he figured now was a good time to stop talking. He focused instead on the traffic creeping out of town, west toward the mountains. The sleet had turned to snow, and was beginning to stick to the browned grass along the roadside.

He exited the freeway onto a county road. The weather would have I-70 traffic slowed to a crawl, so this rural route would probably be faster. "I remember traveling this way once with my mother when I was about twelve," Andi said, apparently having decided that, even though he was a man, he was worth talking to.

"Where were you headed?" Simon asked.

"My uncle has a cabin in South Park." She smiled. "The real South Park—the one the show was named after."

"Just a mother-daughter getaway?"

"Not exactly," she said. "At the time I didn't realize it, but looking back, I think she and my father had had an argument of some kind and she wanted to get away for a few days, so she took me to stay at the cabin. It was all a novelty to me—a woodstove for heating and cooking, a hand pump for water and a little log outhouse. We hiked and fished and roasted marshmallows over a campfire." She smiled. "Living with the Family reminded me of those times."

"When was the last time you were there?" Simon asked.

Her smile faded. "About six months before my mother died. My uncle still has it, but he only uses it for a few weeks during hunting season. Maybe I'll go back one day." She rubbed her belly. "I'd like to show it to my son or daughter."

The baby. Something else for him to worry about. The doctors had said she could deliver any time now. "How are you feeling?" he asked.

"I need to use the bathroom."

He spotted a sign for a gas station up ahead and signaled to pull in. The snow was heavier now, fat white flakes clumping on the windshield and clinging to the branches of the evergreens that lined the road.

"Take your time," Simon said as Andi climbed out of the cruiser. "I'm going to fill up while we're here."

After he filled the tank, he pulled into a parking spot near the door and went inside. He bought coffee, then lingered by the hot plate. When Andi came out of the restroom, he'd ask her if she wanted anything.

"It's nasty out there," the man behind the counter said. Simon judged him to be in his fifties, his hair in a long silver braid down his back, fastened with multiple rubber bands.

"Mmm." Simon turned back toward the restrooms, not interested in small talk.

"They're saying it's going to get worse before it gets better," the clerk said.

Simon suppressed a sigh. Now if he didn't talk to the guy, he would call even more attention to himself. He would be that rude guy who was too snotty to make conversation. "That's pretty much what they always say, isn't it?" he said.

The man laughed. "You're right about that. Where you headed?"

"Breckenridge," Simon said. The popular ski town was the opposite direction of where he intended to travel.

"They'll be excited to see snow this early," the clerk said. "Not enough to ski on yet, but it's coming."

Andi emerged from the ladies' room and moved toward Simon. He realized he was staring again—something he did too often when he was around her—and made himself look away. "Do you want something?" he asked, holding up his coffee cup.

She looked around, grabbed a granola bar and handed it to him, then added a package of nuts. "I get hungry," she said, a little defensively. "I'm eating for two."

"I imagine you do." He should have thought of that before now. He added a second pack of nuts. "So do I, and I'm only eating for one."

He paid for their purchases, and the clerk slid his change across the counter. "You folks have a good time in Breck," he said.

"In Breck?" Andi asked when they were in the car. "What did he mean by that?"

"He asked where we were going, and I told him Breckenridge."

"Why did you lie?"

"In case someone comes along after us and asks where we were headed."

"You mean Daniel. You shot him. He's probably in the hospital somewhere. You don't really think he'll come after us."

"I don't see any reason to take chances."

His phone rang, and he checked the display. A Denver number. "Hello?"

"Sergeant Daley, Denver Police. Is this Simon Woolridge?"

"Speaking."

"I've got an update for you on your fugitive."

"I've got you on speakerphone with Ms. Daniels, in my car. Do you have Daniel Metwater in custody?"

"Not such good news as that. He sought treatment at an emergency clinic near downtown, using a fake ID. He had an Oklahoma driver's license in the name of David Michaels. The clinic treated him, then phoned us to report the gunshot wound. That's when they found out he was wanted. He ran out a back door before they could stop him."

"Any idea what he's driving?" Simon asked, making a quick check of the other vehicles in the gas station parking lot.

"No," Daley said. "In any case, he's probably ditched it and stolen something else. Easy enough to do—first real cold spell and everybody leaves their car idling while they run into the convenience store to grab a cup of coffee or pay for their gas. Anyway, I thought you'd want to know he's still in the area. And we're looking for him."

"Thanks."

Simon ended the call and turned to Andi. She looked pale but resolute. "I heard everything," she said. "He's coming after us, isn't he?"

"That's what we have to assume." He shifted the cruiser into gear. "But he's not going to stop us. Not if I can help it."

Chapter Seven

Victor drummed his fingers on the steering wheel as he inched his car forward in the bumper-to-bumper traffic. The heavier the snowfall, the slower the traffic crawled, until they were hardly moving at all. This was Colorado—people here were supposed to know how to drive in this weather. He ground his teeth in frustration, pain throbbing behind his eyes.

Between trailing the ambulance to the hospital and getting an update on Andi's condition, staking out the hospital parking lot, then following her and Officer Woolridge back to the hotel, he had grabbed only a few hours of sleep in the front seat of his rental car.

He had stolen this one only an hour before, just in case Woolridge had somehow figured out his identity—or one of his many aliases. The traffic and weather made tailing the cop more difficult. He had thought he would have a chance to grab Andi when they stopped for gas, but Woolridge stayed too close to her.

On the seat beside him, his phone rang. It was the sound of an old-fashioned phone, the kind almost no one seemed to own anymore. He glanced at the screen, wanting to ignore the caller, but the number belonged to a man who could not be ignored. He picked up the phone and swiped his finger across the screen. "What?"

"What's this about Metwater being shot?" The boss sounded annoyed, but then, he always sounded disgruntled. Life irritated him. "Did you shoot him?"

"What are you talking about?" Victor swerved to avoid rear-ending the car in front of him, which had slammed on its brakes.

"We have a contact in the Denver PD. They said Metwater was shot last night. Not dead. Wounded."

Victor grunted. "Where did this shooting take place?"

"The Brown Palace Hotel. I thought you had the place staked out."

"I did." How had he missed Metwater? He knew the answer to that one—because the cop, Woolridge—had blocked him. "He was there for the woman," Victor said. "He tried to cut her throat. I knew I was right."

"Is she dead?"

"No. I'm following her right now."

"Why are you following her? You should be going after Metwater."

"He'll come back for her."

"Or he'll be smart and head for Mexico."

"When was he ever smart?"

"If you were smarter, you'd have him by now."

Victor ground his teeth together until his jaw ached. "I'll get him," he said. "He's going to come back for her. She has everything he needs. She's rich and he needs money to get out of the country."

"He has money. He has a million dollars that belongs to me."

"I don't think he does have it—not where he can get to it. If he did, he would have used it by now."

"No, he doesn't have it," the boss agreed. "I have men watching the bank where he keeps it. He hasn't come to get it. He hasn't sent any-one else with the key either."

"Then that means he doesn't have the key," Victor said. "Or he knows you're watching the bank."

"He doesn't know. The men I put on the job are very good. They're invisible."

"Then he doesn't have the key. He needs the key to get to the money."

"Then where is the key? The cops tore his place apart. They haven't come for the money either, so they don't have it. Or if they do, they don't know what it's connected to."

Victor squinted through the thick cascade of snow collecting on the hood of his car. "Maybe the woman has the key. Maybe that's why he's so anxious to get to her."

"Then get the woman—and get the key. And get Metwater."

"I'm following her right now," Victor said.

"I'm going to get her, and I'll make sure Metwater knows it. He'll come after her."

"How are you going to get her? Didn't you say she has a cop protecting her?"

"You don't think I can handle one lousy cop?"

"All I've heard from you so far is a lot of talk. I want action. I want Metwater. I want him dead. And I want the million dollars he stole."

"You'll have him. Dead. And you'll have the key." He ended the call and clutched the steering wheel with both hands, squinting through the thick snowfall. The more he thought about it, the more it made sense to him that Andi Matheson had the key to the safe-deposit box where Metwater had stashed the stolen money. The Prophet had sent her away not to safeguard her, but to keep the cops from getting their hands on the key and the money. Metwater had planned all along to meet up with her, collect the cash and get out of town. But the cops had been one step ahead of him.

And Victor was one step behind. But he wouldn't stay behind. He would catch up with the woman and force her to give him the key. Then, when Metwater showed up, he wasn't just going to kill the lying cheat, he was going to make him suffer. Payback for all the trouble Victor was going to now.

ANDI STARED OUT the windshield at the curtains of white flakes coming down, obscuring the road. "Is it even safe to drive in this?" she asked.

"We're fine," Simon said. "As long as the road stays open, I can drive."

"I guess cops are trained in things like that," she said. "Driving in adverse conditions."

"Not really," he said. "But I grew up in Colorado. I know how to drive in snow."

"I grew up here too, but I'm not crazy enough to take my car out in this."

"I guess I am."

He was teasing her—she got that now. He had a very dry sense of humor that some people probably didn't appreciate, but she liked that he didn't joke around and try to humor her. Her father and his friends had been like that—making light when she tried to discuss serious matters with them. Too often, it came across as either patronizing or shallow. Simon wasn't either of those things.

She looked out the window again. "At least no one is going very fast," she said. The line of cars crept along on the snow-covered highway, brake lights barely visible in the whiteout.

Simon glanced in the rearview mirror. "It makes it easier to spot someone following us," he said.

"I don't see how Daniel could find us," she

said. "He was running away from that clinic when we were leaving the Brown Palace."

"He probably guessed that we were headed back to Montrose," Simon said. "I should have thought of that and taken a different route."

She looked around them at the cars on either side, behind and ahead of them, drivers hunched over the steering wheel, peering through the blizzard. No one even glanced her way. "Well, I don't see anyone following us," she said.

"I do," he said.

She froze in the act of reaching for her cup. "Who?"

"Don't look," he said. "But there's a white Kia two cars back. He's been with us since the gas station."

"Just because he's traveling in the same direction as we are doesn't mean he's following us." She fought the urge to look back over her shoulder. "Is it Daniel?"

"I can't tell." Simon checked his mirrors again. "I'm pretty sure it's a man, but beyond that, he's too far back and the snow is too heavy for me to make a positive ID."

"What are you going to do?" she asked.

"Wait a while, see if I can figure out what he's up to."

"What do you mean 'what he's up to'?"

"If he's simply following to see where we go, that's not much of a threat. If he's going to try to intercept us—to get to you and maybe to kill me—then I'll need to try to stop him before he acts."

"How can you possibly know what he's going to do before he does it?"

"I can see how aggressively he tries to keep up with us, what kind of maneuvering he does." He nodded ahead of them. "Once we head up toward Kenosha Pass, the traffic will thin. It will be tougher for him to keep other cars between us. The weather won't allow him to get too far back, or he'll risk losing us. He'll have to show his hand."

Snow crunched under their tires as they wound their way up a series of switchbacks toward the pass. Towering evergreens draped in snow crowded in on either side of the highway, and a few log cabins, smoke puffing from their chimneys, were visible in the distance. The windshield wipers beat steadily, clearing snow from the windshield even as it piled up on the road.

The road widened and Simon pulled to the right, slowing the cruiser. A truck passed them, and then the white Kia. Andi stared at the driver. "That's not Daniel," she said, the tension in her chest easing. "His hair's too light, and that guy had a beard."

Simon scowled. "Maybe I was wrong. Or maybe Metwater has an accomplice."

"Or maybe he's a stranger who was never following us at all."

Simon sped up again. "Are you sure you didn't recognize him?"

She wanted to lie, to tell him she had never seen the man before in her life. But he had been right when he said she was a lousy liar. "He looked familiar to me," she said. "Though I can't think of where I've seen him. But that still doesn't mean he was following us."

"I never got a good look at him. Or his license plate. Snow was covering it, though the cop in me wonders if that was intentional."

"You don't trust anyone, do you?" she asked.

"I'm in a profession that teaches you not to trust."

They reached the top of the pass. Eighteen wheelers were parked on either side of the summit, drivers adjusting chains, or maybe just waiting out the worst of the storm. They started down the long curve that descended into the high-altitude expanse of open prairie known as South Park. Brake lights shone crimson ahead of them, then the vehicle they were following suddenly swerved sideways, and came to rest straddling the road just where it narrowed to two lanes again.

"What is he doing?" Andi asked, as the driver's door opened and a figure raced to the side of the road.

Simon braked, the cruiser fishtailing wildly on the icy road. Andi screamed as the cruiser slid into the side of the stopped Kia, the tortured scream of twisted metal mingling with her own high-pitched cries.

Chapter Eight

Pain exploded in Simon's nose, Andi's screams filling his ears as he tried in vain to see what was going on. The screams stopped—which sent panic through him. He fought to push aside the mass of the airbag, which had expanded on impact and crashed directly into his nose, which was now streaming blood. "Andi!" he shouted. "Are you all right?"

He groped to his right and came into contact with something soft—her shoulder. "I'm okay," she said.

"The baby?"

"The baby's okay too."

The airbags began to deflate. Simon pushed his aside, then shoved Andi's out of the way as well. "Are you sure you're okay?" he asked, resisting the temptation to examine her for broken bones.

"I'm fine. Really."

She did look fine, calmer than he would have thought. "Your nose is bleeding," she said.

He touched his nose and winced. He felt along the ridge. "I don't think it's broken," he said. "Just bruised. Better than a broken head if the airbag hadn't inflated."

"Right."

"Wait here," he said, unfastening his seat belt.

Andi gripped his arm. "What are you doing?"

"I'm going after him." He stepped from the cruiser and almost fell, feet sliding on the ice and snow that caked the road. Daylight was fading fast, the snow still coming down in a curtain, piling up on the shoulders of his coat and clinging to his eyelashes. He saw no sign of the driver of the Kia. A faint trail up the side of the road, heading into an empty field, might have been made by him, but the snow was filling it in fast. Running after him would mean leaving Andi alone. Maybe that was what the man wanted. Maybe there was someone in another car waiting to grab her as soon as Simon was out of sight.

Bracing himself on the side of the cruiser, he made his way to the front and surveyed the damage. The pipe grille guard welded to the front of the vehicle had protected it from the worst of the damage. One headlight was broken and the license plate dangled by a single screw, but other than that, it looked okay. The engine still ran, though the air bags would have to be replaced.

The Kia hadn't fared so well. The impact had

sent it sliding toward the ditch, its side caved in, windshield shattered. It sat, halfway in the northbound lane, canted onto the passenger side. A quick check showed no one inside—no luggage or papers or anything to identify the driver, though he had left the keys dangling in the ignition. The swirl of red-and-blue lights reflected on the snow, and Simon turned to see a county sheriff's SUV creeping toward them. The window rolled down and a young, clean-shaven deputy looked out. "What happened?" he asked.

"The Kia slid to a stop in the middle of the road." Simon indicated the wrecked car. "I couldn't stop on the ice. The driver bailed out just before I plowed into him."

"Where's the driver now?" the deputy asked.

"I don't know." Simon started walking back toward the cruiser.

The deputy pulled alongside him and squinted

at the emblem on the driver's door. "The Ranger Brigade," he said. "What the heck is that?"

"It's a multiagency task force based in Black Canyon of the Gunnison National Park," Simon said. "We deal with crime on public lands."

The deputy nodded. "I think I've heard of you guys. That case in the spring with the FBI agent who was murdered by that senator?"

"That was us," Simon said. He glanced toward the cruiser. Andi sat quietly, smart enough to wait in the vehicle. He hoped she hadn't heard the deputy's comment. The FBI agent had been the father of her baby, the senator her father. The whole thing had been a nasty business, and she had been caught in the middle.

"Is your passenger okay?" the deputy asked.

"Shaken up, but fine," Simon said.

"What about you? Is that blood on your coat?"

"Busted my nose when the airbag deployed. I'm okay." In the cold, the bleeding had stopped quickly.

"Your vehicle looks okay to drive," the deputy said. "But that Kia is totaled." He left the lights going and climbed out of the car. "We'd better look for the driver. He gets lost out here, and he could freeze to death before morning."

Simon made no comment. He had a feeling the driver had someone waiting to pick him up—perhaps up the hill at the top of the pass. Maybe he had hoped to grab Andi in the confusion after the wreck, but the arrival of the county cop had scared him off.

"Do you have a description for me?" the deputy asked.

Simon shook his head. "I never got a good look at him, with all the snow."

"Guess I'd better see some ID from you," the deputy said.

Simon showed his badge, and braced himself for the inevitable question, which the deputy asked next. "What brings you to our side of the divide, Agent Woolridge?"

"I'm following up on a case."

The deputy glanced at Andi. They were close enough now that he could clearly see she was pregnant. He was going to ask about her next, and Simon wasn't in the mood to explain. "It's cold out," he said. "I'd like to get the young lady to someplace safe for the night, and take my car to a repair shop."

The deputy glanced behind them, up the pass. "Denver would be the best bet to get those airbags replaced, but you won't be going there tonight," he said.

"Why not?" Simon asked.

"The pass is closed. You were probably the last vehicle through before we put the gate down." He gestured ahead of them. "It's socked in on both sides of the pass. Ground blizzards can ice up the road, and we get people sliding off left and right. Better for everybody to close it."

"We can't spend the night here," Simon said. Alone, he wouldn't have cared so much, but Andi couldn't spend the night sitting up in a freezing car.

The deputy scratched his chin. "You can try to make it to Fairplay. We'll have a wrecker here in a bit to get this Kia out of the way, and you can follow him."

"It doesn't look like we have much choice."

"Pull your vehicle over to the side there and put on your flashers. I'll radio for some help."

Simon climbed into the cruiser and put it into gear. "What's going on?" Andi asked.

"The road behind us is closed now. We're going to wait here for a wrecker that's coming to deal with the Kia, then we'll follow it to

Fairplay, a little town up ahead." He had passed through Fairplay a few times on his way to and from Denver, but he didn't remember much about it, except that it was small and not close to much else. "Are you warm enough?" Simon asked. She had the coat pulled tightly around her. "I can turn up the heater."

"I'm fine. The coat isn't my style, but it's warm."

"What do you mean, it's not your style?"

"Daniel bought it for me. He thought it was what I should wear."

"But you don't like it."

She shrugged. "It's too flashy and conspicuous. I hate standing out."

"I don't think a woman like you can help standing out."

"If I'm supposed to be flattered by a comment like that, I'm not." There was no missing the chill in her words.

Strike out for Simon. He leaned his head back and closed his eyes, fatigue dragging at him. He hadn't slept more than a few hours in the past twenty-four, and that had been sitting up in the chair in Andi's hospital room. As soon as he had Andi safely settled for the night, he was going to pass out.

He must have dozed off for a few minutes, because he jerked awake to a loud, beeping noise and had to hit the wipers to clear the windshield of snow. A massive orange snowplow was crawling down the road toward them, followed by a wrecker, lights strobing. "The deputy must have called the snowplow too," he said. "Good thinking."

"You must be exhausted," Andi said. "I hope we can find a hotel room in Fairplay."

"We'll find something." If he had to drain his bank account to bribe someone to give them a room, he would do it.

The wrecker winched the Kia up onto the

flatbed while the plow turned around. Simon pulled his cruiser in behind them, and they headed south at a crawl. Even with the plow scraping the road surface and spreading sand, the trip was treacherous. Whirlwinds of snow swirled in front of the cruiser, rocking the vehicle and obscuring the way ahead. Simon hunched over the steering wheel, gripping it until his knuckles ached, focused on the dull red glow of the wrecker's taillights and hoping the driver didn't slide off the pavement, taking Simon with him. Beside him, Andi was rigid, and absolutely silent.

After what seemed like an hour, but was probably only twenty minutes, the wrecker signaled a right turn. The wind had died and the road was less icy. Simon followed him onto the main street of Fairplay, Colorado. Through the curtain of snow, he could just make out the lighted signs of the businesses along the town's main street—a real estate office, bank, liquor store and taxidermist.

"That was horrible," Andi said. "I thought we would slide off the road—and maybe off the side of a mountain—at any minute."

"I knew we'd be fine," Simon lied.

"What do we do now?" she asked.

He spotted a large lit-up sign. The red letters spelled out *Hotel*. "I think we get a couple of rooms for the night."

THE FOOTE HOTEL reminded Andi of a grand-mother's house—if her grandmother had gone for moose heads, bear skins and cozy, flowered furniture. A string of cowbells on the door an-nounced their arrival as she and Simon stepped into a wood-floored front room. Heat from the fire blazing on a stone hearth blasted them— she was so tired she could have stretched out on one of the chintz-covered sofas and fallen asleep with only her coat for a coverlet.

A tired-looking, genial-faced man looked up from behind a counter. "Nasty night out," he said.

"Do you have any rooms?" Simon asked.

"We've got one room left. Grandpa Foote. It has two beds and a private bath. The rate includes a full breakfast in the morning."

"We'll take it." Simon pulled out his wallet and handed over some bills.

"Where you folks from?" the man asked.

"Denver," Simon said. "Apparently, the road closed behind us."

"You're lucky you made it through." He handed over Simon's change and an old-fashioned key on a brass fob. "The room is at the end of the hall on the left. If you need anything, I'm Mike, the manager."

"It's such a charming hotel." Andi slid her hand along the back of a polished oak rocker. "Has it been here a long time?"

"Since the thirties," Mike said. "Some people say we're haunted, if you're interested in that kind of thing."

"Haunted?" Andi gaped at him, sure he must be teasing her.

"People say they've seen Grandpa Foote rocking in that chair there. And there's a young man who supposedly walks around upstairs, but personally, I don't believe in ghosts."

"I don't either," Andi said, but she moved her hand away from the back of the rocker.

"Is there any place close we can get some dinner?" Simon asked.

The hotel manager glanced over at Andi. She must have looked as bad as she felt. "I've got some lasagna left over from a dinner I catered," Mike said. "I can fix plates for you, eight dollars each."

"That sounds wonderful," Andi said before Simon could answer. "Thank you."

"You go on up and I'll bring it up to you," Mike said.

Simon went out to fetch their bags. "Where are you headed?" Mike asked.

"Breckenridge," Andi said.

"With snow like this, the ski resort will be opening soon," Mike said. "Could be the earliest opening in a while."

"Do you ski?" Andi asked, more to be polite than because she was interested.

"Over a hundred and thirty days last year," Mike said.

Simon returned and led the way up the wooden stairs, which creaked loudly as they made their way up. Each room had a name as well as a number—School House, China Jane, Nature. Grandpa Foote, at the end of the hall, featured two iron bedsteads covered with patchwork quilts, a rocking chair and a bathroom with an old-fashioned white cast-iron tub on claw feet.

Andi stared at the rocking chair. "Do you believe in ghosts?" she asked.

"No." He set down their bags and shed his coat. "But I believe they probably make a good marketing hook for tourists. Do you want to change clothes or anything before we eat?"

"A hot bath sounds so good," Andi said, hugging her arms across her chest.

"Go ahead," he said. "I'll let you know when the food gets here."

She felt self-conscious, undressing with Simon just on the other side of the door. He was still the cop who had harassed the people she cared about for the past months—but she was beginning to see other sides to him. The memory of waking up in the hospital to find him by her side stirred something in her. He made her feel vulnerable in a way she hadn't allowed herself to feel since her mother's death. As much as she had cared for Daniel, their relationship had always been about him—what she could do for him, what he needed from her.

Simon was different. He didn't seem to expect anything of her, and seemed more concerned for her comfort than his own.

She stepped into the warm bath water, sighing as it flowed over her body. She smoothed her hands over the taut mound of her belly, smiling as the baby shifted at her touch. This little life inside her had transformed her, from a woman whose whole identity was defined by her looks and her position in society, to someone who scarcely ever thought about such things. She hadn't looked in a full-length mirror in months. Her body had changed, but her way of thinking had changed, also. All the things that used to matter to her—clothes and shopping and parties—felt silly and empty now. The most important thing was providing a good, safe life for her child.

She thought she had found that safety with the Prophet, but obviously she had been wrong. She touched the necklace, the rough surface of the diamond and the smooth warmth of the gold. She had lied when she had told Daniel she took it as a way to feel closer to him. She had taken it because she was angry with him for cheating on her with other women. She looked at the necklace as payment for the grief he had put her through. Part of her had even been disappointed that he hadn't been more upset by her theft of the piece. He had actually seemed happy for her to have it.

She slid her hand up to her throat, and touched the rough lines where the knife had cut her. It seemed so unreal—a terrible nightmare. That a man she had loved could do such a thing…a chill ran through her in spite of the heat from the bathwater.

From there her mind drifted to the Kia driver who had followed them. He had looked so familiar to her, but she couldn't place him. Who did she know who was blond with a beard? Not a beard, exactly—more like a goatee.

The image of the man by the elevator in the Brown Palace, the one with the Russian accent, made her sit upright, water sloshing over the side of the tub. But why had he been following them?

When she emerged from the bathroom, dressed in a loose gown and robe, Simon indicated a tray that sat on an old-fashioned wooden chest of drawers. "Mike just brought up the food," he said.

Her stomach cramped with hunger. "I'm starving." She started to lift the tray, but Simon intercepted her.

"Sit in the rocker," he said. "I'll bring it to you."

"You don't have to wait on me," she protested.

"I do," he said. "Otherwise, my mother might come back to haunt me. She was a Southern belle from Atlanta and believed in old-fashioned manners."

She smiled at the idea of this stoic, rather severe lawman being schooled by his mother to say *Yes, ma'am* and hold open doors. She settled into the rocker and he brought a plate to her. The aroma of the lasagna made her mouth water, and she feared her own manners suffered as she devoured it, as well as the salad and bread that accompanied it.

Hunger sated, she looked across at Simon. Head down, his shoulders drooped, as if they carried a burden that was too heavy. She should tell him that she thought the driver of the Kia had been the Russian, but what could he do about that now? It would only make him worry. He might even try to go out in the storm to search for the man. She would tell him tomorrow, after they had both had a chance to rest. "Why don't you take a bath now and I'll carry the dishes down," she said.

"I can take them down," he said, starting to rise.

"No, please." She stood and added his plate to hers on the tray. "I'd like to stretch my legs, after sitting in the car all day."

"I should go with you," he said.

"Oh please," she said. "Who's going to bother me here? With the snow and the roads closed, no one can reach us here—if they could even find us. And you'll feel better after a bath. It will take the chill off."

"All right." He rubbed the back of his neck. "The hot water would feel good."

He went into the bathroom, and she gathered the dishes on the tray and headed downstairs. She found Mike in the kitchen. "Dinner was delicious," she said, as he hurried to take the tray from her. "Thanks so much. I wasn't looking forward to going back out in that storm."

"Glad you enjoyed it." He carried the dishes

to the sink at the back of the kitchen, and she followed him a few steps inside. "If you need anything else, let me know," he said. "I remember when my wife was expecting our kids, she would get hungry a lot."

"I do that too." She smiled, relaxed for the first time in a long while.

"When are you due?" he asked.

"I have another couple of weeks, I think," she said. The doctor had told her the baby could be born any time now, but she didn't want to worry this nice man. And she felt fine. A little awkward and uncomfortable, maybe, but she had felt that for months.

"Tough time to travel," Mike said. "Do you have family in Breckenridge?"

The question puzzled her, then she remembered that she and Simon were supposed to be on their way to Breckenridge. If she lied and said yes, she had family there, Mike might ask their names, and that would lead to a whole other mess of lies. "No. Simon has business there and we didn't want to be apart, with my due date so close." That sounded better—all sweet and romantic, even.

"I remember when my first was born, I felt that way too," he said. "I didn't want to let my wife out of my sight."

She swallowed past the sudden tightness in her throat. If only someone really felt that way about her. It sounded so nice. Instead of someone who loved her watching over her every move, she was being stalked by a man who wanted to do her harm.

The bells on the front door jangled and Mike looked in that direction. "I'd better go see who that is," he said.

"Is it all right if I make tea?" she asked, indicating the tea and coffee service on the table just outside the door.

"Help yourself," he said, and moved past her into the front room.

She selected a tea bag and filled a mug with hot water, then stood waiting for it to brew before she added sugar.

"Do you have a room for the night?" The familiar voice, with its softly accented tones—definitely Russian—sent a chill through her.

"Sorry, but we're full," Mike said.

"I don't require anything fancy," the voice said. "My car broke down, and I hitchhiked into town. The other places I asked said they were full too."

Scarcely daring to breathe, Andi tiptoed to the door that separated the dining area from the front room and peered out. The blond with the goatee who had addressed her by name at the Brown Palace stood across from Mike. He wore a stocking cap and a dark blue ski jacket, but it was the same man, she was sure.

"I can let you sleep on the sofa," Mike said, indicating the chintz-upholstered furniture in front of the fireplace. "That's the best I can do."

"I would be so grateful. Do you have a restroom I could use?"

"Right over there." Mike pointed to the men's room.

As soon as the blond closed the door to the men's room behind him, Andi left the dining room and headed for the stairs.

"Did you change your mind about tea?" Mike called after her.

"Yes. Thank you," she said, and all but ran up the stairs to the room at the end of the hall. She shoved her key into the lock with shaking hands and pushed open the door.

Simon emerged from the bathroom, bare chested, toweling his hair. "Everything okay?" he asked.

She sank onto the bed, her wobbly legs unable to support her. "There's a man d...downstairs," she managed to stammer. "He just came in. I'm sure he's the man who was talking to me at the Brown Palace—the one by the elevator who knew my name."

"You're sure it's the same man?" Simon asked.

She nodded. "He has an accent—Russian, I think."

Simon sat beside her, not touching her, but his presence so close steadied her. "I'm wondering now if he was the man in the Kia," she said. "I think I recognized him."

"It might have been him," Simon said. "Did he see you?"

"I don't think so. I was in the kitchen. I overheard him talking to Mike, then I peeked around the door. It was definitely him."

"What did he say?"

"He said he wrecked his car and had to hitchhike to the hotel. He looked pretty cold, but not too frozen. Mike told him he could sleep on the sofa by the fire, since all the rooms are full. He went into the restroom and I hurried up here."

She gripped Simon's arm. "What are we going to do? We can't leave without him seeing us, and where would we go in all this snow?" Her throat tightened and she fought down panic. When they had left Denver, she had thought they were safe. Instead, they had ended up in a worse predicament. "We're trapped here—with a man who probably wants to kill us."

Chapter Nine

Simon's first instinct was to hustle Andi into the car and drive to safety, but common sense overruled that impulse. They were both too exhausted to go anywhere that night, and in this weather he was as likely to drive off the side of a mountain as to reach his destination safely. He reached for his shirt. "I'm going downstairs to check him out," he said. "Lock the door behind me and don't let anyone in."

"All right." Andi's lower lip trembled, but she steadied herself. "Be careful."

"Always."

He finished dressing, then tucked his pistol in the waistband of his pants and covered it with a loose shirt. Only a pale glow guided him as he descended the stairs. The kitchen and dining areas, as well as the check-in counter, were dark and there was no sign of Mike. A fire blazed in the hearth, and a lone man sat on one of the sofas facing the fire. He turned to look at Simon.

"I didn't expect to find anyone else up," Simon said.

The man rose from his seat, the light from the fire throwing his face half in shadow, giving it a sinister cast. "What are you doing here?" he asked.

Simon moved closer to the man he had confronted in the Ship Tavern bar—was it really only last night? It felt like ages had passed. "I'm spending the night here out of the snow," he said. "What are you doing here?"

"The same." He couldn't see the man's face

well enough to read his expression in the dim light. "The manager is allowing me to stay down here tonight," he said.

"You've been following me," Simon said.

"I understand paranoia is one of the first signs that one is losing his grip on reality," the Russian said.

"You were driving the Kia that caused us to crash," Simon said.

"I don't know what you're talking about." He glanced up the stairs. "Is Miss Matheson with you?"

"Why do you want to know?"

He shrugged, an overly casual gesture that didn't fool Simon. "It would be good to say hello to an old friend."

"She doesn't want to talk to you."

"How is it your business who she talks to?"

Simon brushed back the tail of his shirt to reveal the gun in its holster and the badge clipped to his belt. "Agent Simon Woolridge. And you are?"

"You may call me Victor."

"Is that your real name?"

Again, the casual shrug.

"Leave Ms. Matheson alone."

"I think you and I are interested in the same person, and it isn't Miss Matheson," Victor said. "I am looking for Metwater. I think you are too."

"Do you know where he is?" Simon asked.

"No. But I think he will come for Miss Matheson. You think so too. That is why you are here."

Simon didn't deny or confirm this. "When I find Daniel Metwater, I'm going to arrest him," he said.

"Not if I find him first."

"I could arrest you for interfering with police business."

"Unlike my homeland, this is a free country," Victor said. "You may not like my being here, but I haven't broken any laws. You can't arrest me."

"Leave Andi Matheson alone," Simon said again.

Victor sat back down, and stretched his arms over his head. "I am tired. I would like to sleep now," he said.

"I'll see you in the morning," Simon said.

"Good night," Victor said. He lay back and closed his eyes.

Simon waited a moment, then turned and started up the stairs. At the landing, he looked back, not surprised to find that Victor had raised his head and was staring after him.

Upstairs, he knocked softly on the door to his room. "Andi, it's me, Simon," he said.

Something scraped across the floor, then the lock turned. The door opened and Andi stood, one hand on the back of a straight wooden chair. Simon sent her a questioning look.

"I shoved the chair under the knob after you left," she said. "I figured it would make it harder for anyone to get in."

"I don't think Victor will make any moves tonight," Simon said. He shut the door behind him and turned the lock.

"Is that his name? Victor? How do you know?" She followed him across the room.

Simon removed his gun and laid it on the bedside table. "I introduced myself, and he told me his name is Victor," he said. "I don't know if it's his real name—probably not."

"You talked to him? What did he say?"

"As little as possible." He sat on the side of the bed and began removing his shoes. "I let him know I was onto him, that he was to leave you alone or there would be consequences."

"Consequences?"

"I promised to protect you, and I will. By doing whatever that requires."

He didn't look up, but he could feel her eyes on him. She had a way of looking at him that made him feel stripped bare, as if she could see past any front he put up and tell what he was really thinking. It was both unnerving and oddly freeing, as if he didn't have to pretend anything with her, because there was no point.

The bed springs creaked as she sat on the other bed across from him. "Maybe it's just a coincidence that he's here," she said.

"He made you uneasy at the Brown Palace," Simon said. "He knew your real name."

"Maybe I really did meet him somewhere before," she said. "I went to a lot of public functions with my father. So many that I lost track of them all. I could have very easily met him and forgotten."

"He said he was looking for Metwater." He

hadn't intended to reveal this to her, but saw no point in hiding the information now.

Her eyes widened. "Why is he looking for him?"

"I don't know. But when I told him I intended to arrest Metwater, he said that wouldn't happen if he got to him first."

"Does that mean he's going kill him?" Her lower lip trembled.

"Maybe. Or maybe he's going to help him get away." Simon didn't think so, but he had been trained to look at every possibility in a case.

"I doubt that," she said. "Daniel didn't like Russians. He was a little afraid of them, even. I always assumed it was because the Russian mob killed his brother."

Simon stifled a yawn. "I'm not going to worry about it now," he said. "He's downstairs, we're up here and no one is going anywhere tonight. The best we can do is try to get some sleep."

Andi glanced over her shoulder, toward the door. He stood and checked the lock, then positioned the chair back under the knob. "I won't let anyone get to you," he said, before returning to the bed closest to the door.

THOUGH HER BODY ached with exhaustion, Andi lay awake in the darkness, every creak of a floorboard setting her heart thumping. In the bed across from her, Simon slept, his breathing deep and even. He must truly believe they were in no danger, to sleep so soundly. Yet her mind refused to let go of her fear. What did the Russian—Victor—want? Was he really the man in the Kia? Was his name even Victor? Why had he followed them?

So many questions, and no answers.

Seeking distraction, she focused on Simon.

Having seen him in camp many times, she thought she had him figured out. He was a tough, by-the-book cop, prejudiced against Daniel Metwater and all his followers, quick to judge and loath to compromise. He was sarcastic, impatient and stubborn.

Having spent most of the last twenty-four hours in his company, she now knew that he was all those things, but also much more. He had shown her nothing but kindness. He had a dry, subtle sense of humor and a compassion that ran deep. He was honest to a fault, and she believed she could trust him with her life.

Beneath his cool, brittle exterior, she sensed a man who judged himself as harshly as he judged others—a man wary of relationships who had nevertheless revealed things to her she sensed he had not revealed to his coworkers or others he called friends.

She was drawn to him, in a way she had

not been drawn to any other man. Though not physically imposing, he had a lean, athletic grace that stirred her. Sometimes when his dark eyes met hers, she felt swoony as a lovesick teen—and aroused as only a mature woman could be.

She felt safe with Simon. Not merely physically safe, but free to be fully herself without judgment. Though he had said more than once that he thought she was beautiful, she sensed he looked beyond surface beauty, to something deeper. He had seen her pale from fear, hollow-eyed from lack of sleep, swollen from pregnancy, with uncombed hair and no makeup, yet none of that made any difference to him. He had touched her just as gently, held her with just as much strength.

Did he know how strongly she was attracted to him? How much she wanted to feel his arms around her just now, to explore the hard plane of his chest with her hands, to trace the lines of muscle in his arms and shoulders?

Clearly, she had found something to distract her from worries over her safety, but now she was anything but sleepy. Not that she expected Simon to do anything about her aroused state, but if she could only lie beside him, she thought she would be able to relax enough to go to sleep. Maybe he would appreciate the company as well. Or, exhausted as he must be, he might not even wake up.

Carefully, she folded back the blankets and sat, wincing as the iron bedstead creaked. She tiptoed across to the bed where Simon slept, the bare wood floors cold against the bottoms of her feet, and lifted the covers, then eased herself in beside him.

He immediately rolled over to face her. She lay on her back, scarcely daring to breathe. Any second now, she half expected him to cry out in alarm, or to send her back to her own bed.

When he spoke, his voice was quiet, nothing like that of a man who had been in a deep sleep. "Andi, what are you doing here?" he asked.

"I couldn't sleep," she said.

He waited, saying nothing.

Tentatively, she reached out and touched his side. He was naked from the waist up, wearing only a pair of boxers. "I thought I would feel safer if I was closer to you."

He rolled toward her and put one arm around her, pulling her to him. She turned on her side, spooning against him. His arm rested under the curve of her belly. "Is that better?" he asked, his breath soft against her neck.

"Yes. It's wonderful." She settled more firmly against him, a breathy cry escaping her as his arousal poked against her bottom.

"Sorry," he muttered, and tried to shift away.

"Don't be." She pressed more firmly against him. When he didn't move away again, she took his hand and brought it up to cup her breast.

He shaped his hand to her and pressed his head against her shoulder. "Have I done that lousy a job of hiding my feelings for you?" he asked.

Her heart sped up. "You have feelings for me?"

"Since the first day I saw you."

"I didn't know," she said. "I was afraid you would think I was being foolish. Or worse—manipulative."

He pressed himself more fully against her. "I deal with a lot of manipulative people in my job. You don't strike me as one of them."

He didn't mention Daniel's name, but he didn't have to. The more time Andi spent apart from the Prophet, the more she saw how he had played her, how he played all his followers. He was very good at figuring out what they needed and giving it to them. He had recognized how lonely and lost she had been, and had given her companionship and direction.

It was as if Daniel had put her in a trance from which she was only now awakening. "No, I'm not trying to manipulate you," she said. "I only want to be with you. Tonight."

When he didn't respond, she reached back and took the hard length of his arousal in her hand. The soft hiss of his breath through his teeth encouraged her. She began to stroke him, gently at first, then with more firmness.

Simon's hand on her wrist stilled her. "You don't have to do this," he said.

"Oh, but I want to," she said. She rolled over to face him, and brought her lips to his.

He didn't hesitate to respond, his lips firm

and caressing. He kissed her gently at first, as if gauging how far she would let him go. When she responded eagerly, he pressed more, teasing apart her lips with his tongue, angling his head to deepen the kiss, setting every nerve ending buzzing with awareness of him.

Her lips still pressed to his, she began stroking him once more. This time, he didn't stop her, but began fondling her breasts, the nipples beading at his touch. "Is this all right?" he asked.

"More than all right," she gasped. She licked her palm, then grasped him once more. He bent to draw one nipple into his mouth through the thin fabric of her gown and she moaned, need thundering through her, her muscles tightening, aching for more.

She started to slide down the length of him, but he pulled her up again. "Just your hands this time," he said.

"Yes," she whispered. She wanted that closeness too, that face-to-face, body-to-body contact—that feeling of being held and carried along with your lover to completion.

She began to caress him again, sliding her fingers down to fondle his balls, varying the pressure and speed of her movements. He buried his face against her neck, his breathing increasing, until he was panting. She wrapped her free arm around him, pulling him against her until she could feel the pounding of his heart. She matched her breathing to his, her own desire winding tighter as he neared his release.

When he came, she cried out as well, and he gripped her tightly to him, kissing her neck, her face and finally her lips, a deep, drugging kiss that left her light-headed and breathless.

He leaned over her and pulled a handful of tissues from the box on the bedside table and cleaned himself. She lay on her side, her head on his chest, listening to the steady beat of his heart. She fully expected him to go to sleep now, as exhausted as he had been earlier. And that was all right. Maybe they would find another time for him to return the favor.

But Simon had other ideas. He tossed the tissues in the trash, then traced his hand along the curve of her body, slipping down lower, until his fingers probed at her entrance.

"Oh!" She let out a cry of both delight and surprise as he slid one finger into her.

"Your turn," he said, and kissed her cheek.

"You don't have—" But the protest died on her lips as he began to stroke and fondle, sliding in and out of her, teasing her with his fingers and thumb. She clung to him, gripping his back as desire shuddered through her. She sighed and gasped, unable to keep quiet as the urgency built. He kissed her lips, then along her jaw, hesitating a moment when he reached the diamond necklace, before moving on to her breasts, sucking and teasing her aching nipples until she was half-blind with need.

She came hard, bucking against him, shutting her eyes tightly and riding the wave of pleasure that rocked her. Simon's hand and mouth stilled and he held her, cradling her against him, strong arms wrapping around her. She kept her eyes closed, breathing in the scent of him, reveling in the pleasure of being surrounded by him, her senses overtaken by Simon.

Eventually, he shifted, pulling his arm from beneath her. She sat up. "Going back to your own bed?" he asked. Was she imagining the disappointment in his voice?

"No, I'm only going to the bathroom."

She returned shortly and slid beneath the covers beside him once more.

"Your feet are cold," he said, as she pressed them against his warm legs.

She smiled, then laughed.

"What's so funny?" he asked.

"Nothing." She couldn't tell him she had laughed because it was such an old married couple comment—or at least it seemed like one to her. In her admittedly limited experience, new lovers never complained about anything, intent on making the best impression. Only long acquaintance made people comfortable enough to voice objections.

But Simon wasn't like that. He never held back his honest opinion. Though neither did he move away from her and her cold feet. She settled her back more firmly against him, his arm draped over her ribs once again. "Good night," she said softly.

He slid his hand up and took hold of the

necklace. "I didn't notice this before," he said. "Where did you get it?"

She stiffened, groping for some lie that would satisfy him. But she couldn't move from being so intimate with him to lying. "It's Daniel's," she said. "I…well, I took it from him."

"Can I take a closer look?"

"I guess so."

He sat and leaned over her to switch on the lamp on the nightstand. "It looks old," he said.

"I think it might be." She had to hold herself back from wrapping her hand around the pendant, trying to hide it.

"It looks like the one Michelle Munson described—the one she said belonged to her foster sister."

"Yes. I guess it might be. I thought maybe Cass gave it to David, Daniel's brother, and that Daniel inherited it when David was killed.

But if it really was Michelle's sister's, I'll give it back to her."

His gaze shifted from the necklace to her eyes. "Why did you take it?" he asked.

"I was angry with him for sending me away. I saw it when I was going through his motor home, gathering things to take with me, and I just took it. I wanted to get back at him, I guess. But it didn't work."

"What do you mean?"

"He saw the necklace when he grabbed me in the hotel room last night. He actually seemed happy that I had it. He said I was his good luck charm."

Simon grasped the pendant. "Michelle said her sister's necklace was a locket. That means it opens, right?"

"Right. But I don't think this one opens. There are no hinges, and I don't see a catch."

About that time the front of the pendant sprang open. "Oh!" she cried. "How did you do that?"

"There's a hidden catch along the side," he said. "See, there's a shallow compartment here." He leaned closer. "There's a key." He held up a flat brass key, notched along one side.

"It's an odd-looking key," she said. "It doesn't look like it fits a door or a car."

"I think it's a safe-deposit box key," Simon said. "Did Metwater ever mention a safe-deposit box?"

She shook her head. "No."

Simon fit the key back in the locket and closed it. "Maybe he didn't know about it. It might belong to his brother. Or to Michelle's sister."

"We can ask her when we see her again," she said. "Whenever that is."

"Tomorrow," Simon said. "I plan on taking

you to the same safe house where she and her son are staying."

She lay back, weariness dragging at her. "That would be good." There were too many unanswered questions in her life right now.

Chapter Ten

Victor lay awake long after the hotel had fallen silent. The clock on the mantle struck a doleful midnight, and he rose and began to pace. The old wood floors creaked beneath his feet and odd drafts swirled in his wake, setting the pages of magazines fluttering and the leaves of potted plants rustling. He added wood to the fire and the blaze roared to life, sparks spiraling up the chimney, the logs popping and crackling. He should have been exhausted, after hours in the cold, trudging miles through the snow before he was able to flag down a passing county truck, the driver astonished to find anyone out on the closed road. By the time he had reached the Foote Hotel, he had been half-frozen and aching for bed.

But his encounter with Simon Woolridge had energized him. He had had no idea Woolridge and Andi were here when he chose this place to stay the night. He just needed a room for one night, and this was the only place he could find. This had worked out great because it saved him having to look for her, but he had to figure out how to get the cop out of the picture so that he could get to Andi. Soon after that, Metwater and the key to a million dollars would be his.

He moved to the kitchen, ignoring the employees-only sign on the door, and headed for the massive commercial refrigerator. He needed fuel for his body and his mind. He opened the door and found a pan half full of lasagna, which he ate with his hands, red sauce staining his fingers and running into his goatee. He grinned at the idea, and grabbed a pint of milk to wash down the culinary carnage. Finished with his meal, he left the empty dish in the sink and washed his face and hands, dripping water on the floor.

He returned to the front room and the crackling fire, and listened for any sound of movement overhead. Wind moaned outside and the old house creaked, but he could detect no sign of life from the occupants of the bedrooms overhead. Behind the front desk, he found an old-fashioned registrar. Apparently the bookkeeping at the Foote Hotel was as antiquated as the furnishings. He flipped to that day's date and found the neat inscription, "Mr. and Mrs. Simon Woolridge." Mr. and Mrs., was it? Another attempt to hide Ms. Matheson's identity? Probably. A woman who would hook up with Metwater didn't strike him as the law-and-order type.

The Woolridges were in the Grandpa Foote room, which the fire plan on the wall showed him was at the very end of the hall. He studied the layout of the hotel with a critical eye. To get to that room from here, he would have to climb the stairs—which creaked. He knew because he had spent the early evening listening to the treads protest loudly with almost every footfall as the various guests made their way up to bed. Then, once he had surmounted the obstacle of the stairs, he would have to traverse a long hallway, which also transmitted the sound of every footstep in amplified clarity. At this time of night, most of the guests would probably wake at his approach, and it was pretty much a given that Woolridge, the wary cop, would as well.

The fire plan indicated every exit in red letters—including one at either end of the long upstairs hallway. Each of these doors opened to an outside balcony, with steps leading down to the street. The doors were probably locked at night, but a survey of the keys stored in a drawer beneath the register revealed one marked Outer Doors. He pocketed this one, then found the key labeled Grandpa Foote and took it as well. Adrenaline buzzing in his brain like good vodka, he moved to the sofa and extracted his pistol from his coat and checked that it was fully loaded. Holding it at the ready in his right hand, he eased open the front door and walked around the side of the building until he came to the stairs that led up to the balcony at the end of the hallway nearest Simon and Andi's room.

These steps were newer and quieter than the ones inside, and the night wind helped hide the sound of his approach. He opened the door with his key, closed it behind him and tiptoed a short five steps to the door marked Grandpa Foote.

An ear to the door revealed the muted rumble of soft snoring. He eased the gun into his coat pocket and pulled out a knife. He would cut Woolridge's throat while he slept, and threaten Andi with the same if she didn't come with him quietly.

The key slid smoothly into the lock, and the knob turned soundlessly. But when he tried to push open the door, it refused to budge. He pushed harder and heard the scrape of wood on wood, and then a woman's startled cry.

Hastily, he retreated toward the deeper shadows near the exit. The door to the room across the hall from Woolridge's opened, and a woman's pale face peeked out. "I told you," she whispered, staring directly at him. She looked over her shoulder, back into the room. "It's the ghost of Grandpa Foote. I told you I felt his presence. I knew he would materialize tonight."

While her face was turned away from him, he darted to the exit and out onto the porch again. He would give the two ghost hunters time to settle down before he tried again. Obviously, Woolridge had barricaded the door from the inside. Victor needed to find a way to draw him out. Then he could slip in and grab Andi.

His thoughts shifted to the fire plan, picturing the layout of the hotel once more in his mind. He could see the red exit signs marked on the little hand-drawn map. But there had been other red letters too, those marking fire alarms—one at each end of the hallway.

He glanced inside and spotted the alarm on the wall. A check of the door across the hall from Grandpa Foote—a room marked as Mountain Man—showed the door shut tight.

The ghost hunters had once more retired. Wasting no time, Victor opened the door, moved to the alarm, jerked open the cover and pulled down the handle. An ear-splitting mechanical shriek filled the hallway as he retreated outside once more.

The door to Mountain Man was the first one to open. "The ghost set off the alarm," a stout woman with short curly hair announced to no one in particular. "I saw him."

No one paid her any attention. The alarm continued to shriek, and soon other guests joined the ghostbusters in the hallway, milling around in pajamas and robes and hastily donned coats and slippers. At last the door to Grandpa Foote opened and Simon emerged.

"What's going on?" he shouted above the murmur of the other guests and the blare of the alarm.

"The ghost set off the fire alarm," the curly-haired woman said.

"I think I smell smoke," another woman added.

"We'd better get out of here," a man said, his hands on the shoulders of a petite woman in a Wonder Woman nightshirt. "A place this old could go up in a flash."

This started an exodus toward the stairs. Victor took advantage of the commotion to slip inside, keeping to the shadows along the wall. With Simon's back still to him, he moved into Grandpa Foote and shut the door behind him.

SIMON PUSHED HIS WAY through the crowd in the hallway, trying to assess the situation as the fire alarm echoed in the enclosed space. Up and down the hall, doors stood open and people milled about. If the building really had been on fire, half of them would be toast by now, but Simon didn't smell any smoke. For that reason alone, he had suggested Andi stay in the room while he checked things out. No sense in her going out in the cold if she didn't have to.

"Did anyone call nine-one-one?" someone asked as the guests crowded onto the stairs.

"Did anyone call Mike?" Simon asked.

"I did," someone else said. "He's on his way."

The fact that the alarm was sounding, but none of the hotel's smoke alarms were going off, made Simon suspect deliberate mischief rather than an actual blaze. He located the alarm on the wall, the door open and the handle forced down. "I don't think there's a fire!" he shouted to be heard above the commotion. "Someone pulled the fire alarm. Probably a kid who thinks he's funny." He recalled doing the same when he was a young teen—and being grounded for a month afterward when his father found out. He tried to shove the handle back up, hoping to shut off the deafening clamor, but it refused to budge.

"The ghost set that off." A woman stopped at his shoulder and scowled at him. "I saw him."

Whatever she had seen, Simon was sure it wasn't a ghost. "What did he look like?" he asked.

"He had white hair and a white beard," she said. "I'm sure it was Grandpa Foote."

"We should go." A man took her arm and tried to move her toward the door, but she stood her ground.

"There's no fire," she said. "The ghost of Grandpa Foote is playing tricks."

Blond hair could look white in the semi-darkness, Simon thought. And hadn't Andi described Victor's goatee as a beard earlier? Cold sweat drenched him as he looked around for the Russian, who was nowhere to be seen in the milling crowd. Cursing himself for leaving Andi, he rushed back to his room.

The door swung open easily at his touch, and he stared into the empty room. Andi's robe lay in a silken puddle by the bed, as if she had been interrupted in the act of putting it on. Cursing himself for a fool, Simon raced outside again. "Andi!" he shouted.

Half a dozen heads turned toward him, their faces blank. "Has anyone seen a very pregnant woman?" he asked. "Blonde, in a white nightgown?"

Mutely, they all shook their heads. He spotted the woman who had told him about the ghost. "This ghost, have you seen him again?" he asked.

She shook her head. "No. He probably won't show himself again tonight. He got what he wanted—everyone up and in a turmoil. He'll be happy now. For a while, at least. That's how the spirits are."

When Simon found Victor, he was going to make him very, very unhappy.

ANDI WAS GETTING really tired of men grabbing her and trying to drag her off. First Daniel, and now this Victor guy. She was going to have to start arming herself or something. But honestly, she had been expecting Simon when the door to her room opened, not the Russian. Before she could even scream, Victor had clamped one hand over her mouth, wrapped the other arm across her chest and dragged her backward into the hall and out the door. She could hardly breathe, he was squeezing her so tightly.

And now she was freezing, the rough boards of the porch icy against her bare feet, an arctic wind cutting through her thin nightgown. The night was pitch-black, with no moon and certainly no streetlights to illuminate the scene. A few people had emerged from the hotel to the street below, but they were oblivious to what was happening right over their heads. There was no way this was going to end well for her, and she had her baby to think of too.

Years ago, she had taken a women's self-defense seminar at her university. About a hundred young women had gathered in a gymnasium while a pair of burly guys demonstrated a dozen ways to fight back against an attacker. Then the women had paired up and practiced a few of the moves, with a lot of giggling and not a great deal of finesse. Andi struggled to remember any of those moves now. Wasn't there something about gouging eyes or trying to break his nose?

She reached up and raked her nails across Victor's face, which only earned a punch to the side of her head that made her ears ring. But it also made her even angrier, and instinct took over from her faulty memory as she kicked her heel back to land firmly between Victor's legs.

The results were both instant and highly gratifying. He let out a strangled moan, released her and dropped to his knees, hands covering his crotch. She stumbled down the stairs and into the street, where she collided with Mike, who was hurrying down the sidewalk toward the hotel. "Hey, there." He steadied her with both hands. "What's going on?"

She shook her head. Explaining now would take too much breath. "Have you seen Simon?" she asked.

"No. I just got here."

She followed Mike inside, to a front room full of other guests. The blare of the fire alarm wasn't as loud down here, the raised voices of the guests almost drowning it out. Mike ignored their questions and marched past them up the stairs, Andi behind him.

They met Simon at the top of the staircase. He was fully dressed, including his coat, his dark brows drawn together in a forbidding expression. "I tried to shut off the fire alarm, but no luck," he said to Mike as he moved down the stairs. Then he spotted Andi and stopped. "Are you all right?" he asked.

She nodded, and started past him. He touched her arm, gently, the slightest brush of his fingers. "Victor?" he asked.

She nodded. "I don't know where he is now. I don't care."

"I thought he had kidnapped you," Simon said.

"He tried, but I got away."

"How?"

She frowned at him. "I'm a lot tougher than

I look. But right now, I'm freezing. I need to get dressed."

"I'll be up in a minute."

She continued upstairs after Mike, while Simon started down again. He was probably going to look for Victor, though she was sure by now he would be gone. There were too many people around at this point for him to attempt to grab her again.

Upstairs, Mike disabled the alarm. "What idiot set this off?" he asked.

"It was the ghost of Grandpa Foote," said the curly-haired woman from the room across the hall, a fuzzy brown robe belted around her solid figure. "I saw him. He was hovering over there, next to his room." She pointed to Andi and Simon's room, the one labeled Grandpa Foote. "Then he moved over and pulled the alarm."

"Why would a ghost pull a fire alarm?" Andi asked.

"They like to cause trouble," the woman said. "Especially for people who are occupying the places they once occupied." She turned back to Mike. "You should consider doing something to appease him. Maybe hang his portrait downstairs in a place of honor or something."

"Thanks for the advice," Mike said. He waited until she and her husband had retreated to their room and shut the door before he turned to Andi. "Any idea who actually did this?"

"I think it was Victor," she said. "The man you let sleep on the sofa. I think I saw him up here right after it happened."

Mike's shoulders slumped. "That's what I get for being a nice guy. Well, as my dad always said, 'No good deed goes unpunished.'"

He glanced down at her bare feet. "You must be freezing. You should go back to bed."

She returned to her room, taking care to lock the door behind her, and fix the chair back in place. She was pulling on socks when someone knocked. "It's me," Simon said.

She tugged up the last sock, tightened the belt on her robe then went to let him in. He was still scowling, and the wind had tousled his hair. She resisted the urge to smooth it back into place. "No sign of him," he said, moving past her and taking off his coat.

She fitted the chair back under the doorknob then sat down on the side of the bed again, pulling the blankets around to cover her knees. Simon paced in front of her. "I should have realized it was a trick to draw me away," he said. "I never should have left you alone."

"I'm not going to accept an apology for something that wasn't your fault." She caught his hand as he passed, and he stopped and met her gaze. "If you had insisted I come with you, instead of leaving me behind in the room, maybe he would have shot you or stabbed you, and then dragged me away anyway. As it is, I'm okay."

He sat beside her, still holding her hand. "What happened?" he asked.

"He came in the room, grabbed me and dragged me out onto the porch. I kicked him where it hurts, he let me go and I ran. I hope he's still hurting."

Simon glanced at the clock. "It's only two thirty. You should try to get some sleep."

"Only if you'll try to sleep too."

He shook his head and started to rise, but she tugged him down beside her once more. "You're not going to help anyone by staying awake until you're dead on your feet," she said. "He's not going to come back here tonight, but if he does, we can set up something so we'll hear him."

"Like what?" he asked.

She looked around the room, and spotted the old-fashioned bowl and pitcher on the dresser. "We'll put those china dishes, plus the glasses from the bathroom, on the chair in front of the door," she said. "If anyone tries to shove it open, they'll fall to the floor and break—or at least make enough noise to wake us."

Simon considered the idea, then nodded. "It's primitive, but effective." He stood and carried the dresser set to the chair, then retrieved the glasses from the bathroom and balanced them so that any movement of the door would send them crashing down. Then he lay beside Andi, still fully clothed.

"Are you going to undress?" she asked.

"No." He reached up and switched off the

bedside lamp. "Go to sleep," he said. "I'll be right here."

Were there any more comforting words in the English language?

And was there anyone more stubborn than this lawman? Andi closed her eyes and settled against the solid, reassuring wall of his back. She had proved tonight that she could defend herself when she had to, but she liked knowing she had this gentle man on her side, a man who was determined to protect her at any cost.

Chapter Eleven

Simon woke with a start, the first gray light seeping beneath the window shade. The memory of where he was—and why—filled him. He turned his head to look at Andi, who lay curled on her side next to him. He clenched his hands into fists, resisting the urge to reach out and touch her, not wanting to wake her. The erotic tenderness of the night before had been so incredible—the kind of experience that changed a person on some level he couldn't name. How was it possible to feel so close to a person he had known for such a short time?

True, they had been acquainted with each

other for months. He had interviewed her in connection with various cases, and studied her as Daniel Metwater's closest follower and perhaps the key to unraveling the mystery of the Prophet.

But all the while, he had been trying, unsuccessfully apparently, to hide his attraction to her. Something about this quiet, beautiful woman drew him in.

He had had relationships with women before, dating one for as long as two years. But he wasn't one to open himself up to other people. His long-time girlfriend had left him because she said she was tired of feeling shut out. It wasn't that he had deliberately excluded her, but he had always been a man who kept his thoughts and feelings to himself.

Somehow, being with Andi was easier. When he did talk, she listened, but he never sensed that she wanted more. The fact that she had made the first move toward intimacy thrilled him.

The rest of the night hadn't been quite so wonderful, of course. When he had realized Victor had gotten to Andi, he had been equal parts enraged and terrified. He had underestimated the Russian's daring, and it had almost cost him everything. He wouldn't make that mistake again.

Andi stirred and opened her eyes. Her lips curved in a sleepy, sexy smile that he felt right in his groin. "Good morning," she said.

"How did you sleep?" he asked.

"Better than I would have thought possible." She rolled onto her back and stretched, her breasts thrusting upward in a way that left him dry mouthed. "How about you? Did you sleep at all after we came back to bed?"

"Some." Trying to sleep fully dressed—

which included his bulletproof vest—wasn't the easiest of propositions. "I dozed a bit."

Her smile faded. "I'd scold you about being so stubborn, but I know it wouldn't do any good," she said. "So it's your own fault if you're miserable now."

"Not all of last night was miserable," he said. He rolled over to face her and propped himself up on one elbow.

Her smile returned, her cheeks flushed pink and eyes sparkling. "No, I'd say the first part of the night was pretty wonderful."

"Only *pretty* wonderful?" He tried to look hurt. "My pride is wounded."

"I'm leaving room for even more spectacular revelations in the future." She smoothed her hand down his arm, eyes heavy-lidded with desire.

He tried to smile at her teasing tone, but he had a hard time pretending there would be any future for the two of them. He couldn't imagine two people from more different worlds, and in any case, today duty had to come before his personal desires. "You're very tempting," he said. "But we really need to get back on the road."

She dropped her hand and sighed. "Somehow, I knew you'd say that."

He sat up on the side of the bed and looked over his shoulder at her. "How are you feeling?" he asked.

"You mean, am I in labor yet?"

"That's not what I asked."

"No, but it's what people usually mean when they ask me that question these days. I know I look like I'm going to pop any minute, but not today, I don't think."

"I promise, that's not what I meant," he said.

"Then maybe you mean, how do I feel about what happened last night?" She sat up also, her body angled toward him, close enough that he could feel her warmth, smell the lingering aroma of her perfume. "I feel wonderful." She met his gaze with a challenge in her eyes. "How are you feeling?"

Conflicted. Not the answer she wanted to hear, or that he would give her. On one hand, this gorgeous woman he had been attracted to for months was apparently attracted to him too. On the other hand, she was a crime victim he was charged with protecting, as well as a very pregnant mother-to-be. His job was to get her to safety, not to indulge in his desire to make love to her as often as possible. And was it even safe to have sex when she was so close to delivering? What if he sent her into labor?

"I'm feeling like I'm a pretty lucky man right now," he said, and kissed her cheek. "And as much as I'd like to stay here in bed with you all day, I think we really do need to get up and get on the road."

She closed her eyes and sighed. "I know. How's the weather out there this morning?"

He walked to the window and pulled up the blinds. Ice rimmed each pane, forming a crystalline frame for the scene outside. Sunlight sparkled on six inches of snow that dressed the trees and fence rails, and covered the mud and dirt—a clean, fresh blanket over the peaceful landscape. "It's beautiful out," he said. "Clear skies and hopefully clear roads."

She threw back the covers on her side of the bed. "I'm starving, but that probably doesn't surprise you."

"Mike promised a full breakfast."

At only a little past seven o'clock, the dining room was empty except for a young woman with curly black hair, who greeted them with a smile. "Sit wherever you like," she said. "We have breakfast burritos this morning, and some fresh banana bread."

There was also cereal, fruit, cottage cheese and half a dozen different breads and baked goods. And coffee—strong, hot coffee served in thick white mugs. Simon and Andi filled cups and plates and moved to a table by the windows.

From this seat, Simon could see into the living room. The sofa was empty, the fire cold. The front door opened and Mike entered, wearing cargo shorts, snow boots and a flannel shirt. He dumped a load of firewood on the hearth and began building a fire.

Simon was halfway through his burrito when the manager entered the dining room. "Good morning," he said.

"Morning." Simon nodded toward the sofa. "I see our Russian friend never came back."

"After the stunt he pulled, he had better not

show his face around here again." Mike jerked a thumb toward the kitchen. "He apparently decided to raid the refrigerator and left a mess. If he ever has the nerve to show his face around here again, I'll be filing charges."

"I hope none of us ever see him again," Andi said. She leaned closer to Simon and lowered her voice. "Where do you think he went?"

"He probably stole a car and is lying low for the time being." He took a sip of coffee.

"But you think he'll be back."

"He wants something you have," he said. "Or, more likely, he wants to get to Metwater through you."

"Daniel has no idea where I am right now," she said. "How could he?"

"You're probably right." But he couldn't shake the feeling—call it a lawman's sixth sense—that they hadn't seen the last of Daniel Metwater.

Andi finished off her burrito and pushed the plate away. "Oh, I'm feeling much better now. That was so good."

"We should get going as soon as we can," he said, finishing up his own burrito. "Get on the road before the weather changes."

She pushed back her chair. "I didn't really unpack last night, so it's just a matter of collecting our things."

"I'll go up and get them," he said. "You stay here with Mike. Have another muffin or something."

"I just might do that."

He took the stairs two at a time, pulling out his cell phone as he climbed. Despite the early hour, he wanted to check in with the commander before he hit the road again. He wasn't surprised when Agent Graham Ellison answered on the second ring. Sometimes Simon wondered if the commander ever slept.

"I guess this means you survived the night," he said.

"Yes, sir," Simon said. He unlocked their room and pushed open the door. "We ran into a blizzard south of Conifer and got into an accident—which I suspect may be deliberate." He explained about the Kia following them and the driver running off into the storm.

"Any idea who it was?" Graham asked.

"I'm pretty sure it was the Russian I told you about yesterday. He introduced himself as Victor, though I suspect that's not his real name. He showed up here after we checked in last night and talked the manager into letting him sleep on the sofa. After midnight, he pulled the fire alarm and when everyone came out of their rooms to investigate, he saw his chance and tried to kidnap Andi Matheson. She managed to fight him off and he fled. But I have a feeling he'll be back."

"What does he want with Ms. Matheson?" Graham asked.

"No idea. Maybe he thinks he can get to Metwater through her. Any word on the fugitive prophet?"

"Nothing. The trail's gone cold, though we're pretty sure he hasn't left the country. We've been watching the borders closely. What did you say this Russian is calling himself?"

"Victor. No last name."

"Wait a minute. I think I have something for you." A brief silence, and then the commander returned to the phone. "I think this is your guy—Victor Krayev. Thirty-five. He's from Moscow, but has been in the United States for the last decade. He's a suspected *Bratva* assassin. He was the first suspect in the murder of David Metwater, but Chicago police were never able to come up with enough evidence to pin the charge on him—if they could have even found him. He apparently moves around a lot, and keeps a low profile."

"Interesting. Is he after Daniel Metwater now? Why?"

"Find the answers to those questions, and you might find him," Graham said.

"He probably figures she's his best link to Metwater, especially since Daniel's trail has gone cold."

"Has she told you anything that implicates Metwater in a crime?"

"Not yet. But she must know something. I don't see any other reason for him to pursue her so doggedly."

"He's going to need money to get out of the country, and Andi is his best source," Graham said.

"And tomorrow she turns twenty-five, and gets access to millions of dollars," Simon said.

"Which Metwater probably thinks she'll be happy to hand over to him."

"You don't think she will?"

"I think the events of the past few days have opened her eyes a lot about Daniel Metwater." He hoped so. He didn't like to think the intimacy the two of them had shared had been a sham—and that Andi still loved the man who had cheated, lied and tried to kill her.

"It could be as simple as him believing she betrayed him by coming over to our side, and he wants retribution."

"Maybe. Either way, I don't think he would give up now. He'll keep coming after her until we stop him."

"How is she doing?"

"Good." *Great. She's the most amazing woman I've ever met.*

"She's not giving you a hard time, then? Still defending Metwater?"

"No. She's starting to realize how he used her." He hoped that was true, anyway.

"Get her to the shelter," Graham said. "It will be easier to keep her safe there."

"That's the plan for today. Oh, and two other things—Andi says Metwater has connections in Mexico. He may try to head there. And she has the locket that Michelle Munson said belonged to her sister. The one that disappeared the day she died."

"How did Andi get a hold of it?" Graham asked.

"She stole it from Metwater." Thinking about it made him smile. "She was angry at him for sending her away and I guess she wanted to get back at him, so she took it."

"Risky move, considering what he's shown of his temper."

"She says he knows she has it. I guess he found out the first time he attacked her at the

Brown Palace. But he wasn't upset. He actually seemed happy about it."

"She could be lying."

"I don't think so, sir. And another thing— there's a key inside the locket. It looks like a safe-deposit box key. Andi didn't know it was there."

"Does Andi know what the key is to?"

"She says not."

Another long silence. Simon tensed. "Sir?"

"I trust your judgment," Graham said. "But be careful."

"Yes, sir."

"All right. I expect to see you in a few hours, then."

"Yes, sir."

He ended the call and finished packing the bags, then carried them downstairs, where he found Andi by the front desk, talking to Mike. "Leaving so soon?" the manager asked.

"We need to get going." Simon laid the key on the desk. "Thanks for everything."

"I was telling Mike about my uncle's cabin," Andi said. "He actually knows where it is."

"Sure I do," Mike said. "It's only a few miles from here, up the road to Wilson Pass. I think his kids still come up there in the summers. One of them—Frankie maybe—had me do some repairs up there last fall."

"Frankie is Uncle Doug's oldest son," Andi said. She looked sad. "I haven't seen any of them in years."

"Maybe you can have a reunion up here sometime," Mike said.

"We'd better get going." Simon touched Andi's arm.

She nodded. "Yes, we'd better."

"Drive safe," Mike said. "Weather reports are predicting more snow this afternoon."

"We'll be careful."

The icy wind hit them like a slap when they stepped onto the sidewalk outside the hotel. "Brrr." Andi pulled her coat tightly around her and headed for the cruiser. Simon stowed their bags in the back, then started the engine and stepped out again to scrape ice from the windshield. He kept alert for any sign of Victor, but at this time of morning the streets were almost deserted. Maybe their Russian friend had found a ride out of town.

"So much for the sun," Andi said as Simon turned onto the highway leading out of town. She leaned forward to peer out the windshield at the gunmetal gray sky. "I think the weatherman was wrong about it waiting until this afternoon to snow again."

"As long as the road stays open, we'll get through," Simon said. Even if Monarch Pass was closed, they could go around. The trip would take longer, but this time he wasn't stopping unless he was forced to.

Andi sat back. "I can't believe Mike knew about my uncle's cabin."

"I guess it's not so strange," Simon said. "Fairplay is a small town."

"I wish I could see it again," she said. She turned toward him, the unasked question plain on her face.

"We don't have time to take a detour," he said. "Especially not with the weather threatening to turn on us."

"I know. I'm just feeling nostalgic because of the baby, I guess." She faced forward once more, hands on her abdomen.

"Maybe you can get back over here when things have settled down more," he said. Why did he feel so rotten for not being able to take her to see her uncle's cabin, even though he knew pushing on was the right thing to do?

"Yes, I should do that," she said. "I'd like for you to see it."

Did that mean she was thinking about a future for the two of them? He pushed the thought away. Once Andi Matheson settled back into her real life of wealth and privilege, he couldn't see her continuing a relationship with a lowly cop.

"What's that light on the dash?" Andi asked.

He glanced down at the orange light at the bottom of the control panel. "Tire sensor," he said. "Sometimes when it's really cold it comes on. I'll check the pressures next time we stop for gas."

"Amazing how smart cars are these days," she said. "All anyone in camp had were old beaters, so I'd forgotten about all the new technology."

"Yeah, it's useful, but it can be annoying too." He slowed for an icy spot in the road, and the cruiser swerved. Simon frowned. Something didn't feel quite right here. "I'm going to pull over and check the tires," he said. "Just in case something is wrong."

He pulled to the shoulder and waited for a car to pass before he got out and walked around the vehicle. Andi lowered the passenger window and looked out. "Everything okay?" she asked.

Simon stared down at the right rear tire. It was definitely low, and deflating quickly. "We've got a flat," he said.

"Did you run over a nail or something?" Andi asked.

"Maybe," he said. "Or maybe Victor wanted to slow us down. I should have thought of that and checked before we left the hotel." He opened the back door and retrieved his coat. "I'll have to change it. It will only take a few minutes. Stay in the car, where it's warm."

He walked around to the back to retrieve the spare and the tire tools. Another car approached, slowing. Maybe a Good Samaritan offering to help. Simon looked up to wave the guy off and had half a second to register Victor's grim face in the driver's seat before the gun the Russian held fired.

The impact of the bullet in his chest knocked him backward. He sank to his knees in the snow, Andi's screams echoing in the still, cold air.

Chapter Twelve

The image of Simon being shoved against the cruiser by the impact of the bullet and his body slumping to the ground paralyzed Andi. "Simon!" she screamed, fumbling for her seat belt, her numb fingers refusing to work. She could no longer see him, the image of him falling flashing over and over in her head.

She looked down, cursing the stubborn safety restraint. She had to get out of here. She had to help Simon.

The passenger door of the cruiser opened and someone grabbed her arm. She stared up into the face of Victor, who leaned over and hit the button to release the safety belt. "Get out," he ordered, and pulled her from the car.

"No!" She tried to resist, but he held her in an iron grip. Her boots slipped on the icy ground as he pulled her toward a battered blue sedan parked behind the cruiser on the shoulder of the road. "What about Simon?" she asked, looking back and trying to see the other side of the cruiser, where Simon had fallen.

"He can't help you now," Victor said. He opened the sedan's passenger door and shoved her inside. "He's dead."

A sob escaped her at the words. She fought against the tears. "He's not dead," she said. "You're only trying to frighten me."

Victor climbed into the driver's seat and slammed the door. "I shot him in the chest," he said. "I saw the bullet hit. I saw him fall. Dead." He pulled onto the pavement and made a sharp U-turn, throwing her against the door of the car. She groped for her seat belt and fastened it.

"Don't try anything," he said, showing her the gun he still held in his right hand. "I've killed women before. I don't have a problem with it."

She believed him, but that wouldn't stop her from fighting back any way she could. "Why did you shoot Simon?" she asked. "Who are you? What do you want with me?"

"You ask too many questions." He glanced in the rearview mirror and signaled a turn back onto Fairplay's main street.

She grabbed hold of the dash to steady herself as he made the sharp turn. The car was an older model, the dash faded and stained, the upholstery ripped. And it reeked of cigarette smoke. It must have been easy to steal, or maybe he thought no one would miss such a heap. "Do you work for Daniel?" she asked. "Did he send you after me?"

Victor laughed, openmouthed, showing yellowed teeth. "That would be a good one, me working for Metwater." He glanced at her, the menace in his eyes making her ice-cold, in spite of the fur coat. "I need to talk to your lover. I am taking you so that he will have no choice but to come to me."

"What do you want to talk to him about?"

"Again with the questions." He shook his head.

"Maybe I already know what you want to know, and I can save you time and trouble," she said.

"I want to talk to him about his brother. What do you know about David Metwater?"

The question surprised her. "Nothing. I never met him. And Daniel never talked about him. Or hardly ever."

"Don't you think that's odd—that he didn't talk about his twin—his identical twin—that he was so close to?"

"It was too painful for him," she said. "His brother's death affected him deeply. It made him change the whole course of his life."

"Yes, it did, didn't it? And you don't find that odd also—for a man to turn his back on wealth and privilege, to go hide in the middle of nowhere, with a band of loyal followers—people he could depend on to do anything to protect him?"

"Losing his brother made him reevaluate the shallow existence he had been living and re-treat to the wilderness, seeking spiritual purity." Daniel had said those words so often she could repeat them by rote—but did she really believe them anymore? Where was the spiritual purity in cheating on her and lying to her and stealing—yes, she could finally admit the truth in Simon's accusations—he had stolen money and other property that belonged to his followers. Daniel had said a lot of good things, but how many of his own words did he really believe?

The look Victor gave her was equal parts pity and disgust. "I see he has fooled you, the same way he fooled so many others."

Yes, she had been a fool. But she was determined to be smarter in the future. "If it's money you want, I can give that to you," she said. "I have money."

"Do you have a million dollars?"

She gasped. "Daniel won't give you a million dollars. He doesn't have that kind of money."

"He has that and more." He slowed to allow a group of schoolchildren to cross the street. The pavement gleamed wetly, the same dull gray as the sky overhead, in which no hint of blue showed. He held the gun low now, out of sight of passersby, but still aimed toward her so that a bullet would cut through her. "What about a key?" he asked. "Did your prophet ever give you a key?"

"What kind of key?"

"A safe-deposit box key. Small, and made of brass."

Like the key inside the locket. "No," she said, hoping the lie didn't show. "He never gave me anything like that."

"What kind of things did he give you?"

"He gave me this coat." But not the necklace. Daniel hadn't given her that—she had taken it.

He stared at the coat, as if he might see through it. The truck behind them honked its horn and Victor pressed down on the gas, sending them shooting forward. "Where are we going?" Andi asked, as the truck sped up and passed them.

"We are going to Breckenridge. That cop told

everyone that's where you were going—though it obviously wasn't true, since you headed out of town in the opposite direction. But Metwater will have heard this is your destination, so he will try to follow you there. I want to make it easy for him to find you."

"What makes you think he will bother to come looking for me?" she asked. "I'm not the only woman he sleeps with, you know."

"Ah. So you are aware he is unfaithful. And yet you still love him. How touching."

She bit her lip to keep from denying that she loved Daniel. She wondered now if her feelings for him had ever been real love.

"Your prophet needs money," Victor said. "The police have frozen his bank accounts, and if he has the key I'm looking for, he won't be able to use it. You are a rich woman. He will come to you for money."

And tomorrow, on her twenty-fifth birthday,

she would be even richer. Daniel knew this. He had even talked about taking her to Mexico or the Bahamas to celebrate—not that she wanted to be anywhere near a beach and bikinis right now. Since she had agreed that all she possessed belonged to the Family—to Daniel—they had both assumed that once she gained control of the trust, the money would become one of the group's assets also. Daniel probably still believed that. He surely wouldn't be able to fathom that a woman who had made such a fool of herself over him for so long would come to see him in a different light.

He wasn't going to touch another cent of her money if she could help it.

"Besides—you are the only woman who is about to have his baby," Victor said. "A man will go to great lengths to keep his child."

She wouldn't tell him that Daniel wasn't the father of her child—that he had no special ties to her baby, even though he had always claimed he wanted to raise the baby as his own. He had claimed a lot of things that she was learning were not true. But if she revealed the truth to Victor, he might not see her as valuable to him anymore. He might decide to kill her, the way he had murdered Simon.

Simon. The memory of him, slumped on the ground, so still, sent a physical pain through her. When she had first met him, back in camp with the Family, she had hated him. She had thought him a cold, unfeeling lawman who only wanted to persecute her and her friends. But she had been so wrong! These past few days, he had treated her with so much kindness. He had been strong, yet gentle, serious, yet surprisingly funny, too.

He had been her friend, and her lover, and the knowledge that he was gone now was almost too much to bear.

PAIN RADIATED FROM Simon's chest, and he had to fight for breath. He struggled back to consciousness, aware of the cold ground beneath him, the hard metal of the car against his head. Gritting his teeth against the throbbing in his chest, he shoved to his feet, then dared to look down at the hole in his coat and shirt—at the deep indentation in his bullet-proof vest where the bullet that had struck him was still lodged.

He put his hand over the area, feeling the bullet and the torn fabric, but no blood. The vest had done its job. He was bruised, but not bleeding. He had had the wind knocked out of him by the force of the impact, but he was still alive.

Andi! Concern for her galvanized him. He spun around and stared at the open cruiser door, and the empty passenger seat. Footprints in the snow told the story of her leaving in another car—but not alone. A clear image of Victor firing the gun stayed with him. But he had never gotten a good look at the vehicle he had been driving—the one that had taken Andi away.

He examined the tracks left by both the driver and the car. Victor had headed back toward Fairplay. Simon would start there.

Ignoring the dull ache in his chest, he returned to his cruiser and stared down at the flat tire. Victor had probably slashed it last night or this morning, then simply waited for Simon and Andi to drive away and followed them, knowing they would eventually have to stop. With a heavy groan, he knelt in the snow and began changing the tire.

Fifteen minutes later, he had the spare in place and had verified that none of the other tires were damaged. He headed back toward Fairplay, watching the roadside for any sign that a car had turned around. Victor may have been trying to fool anyone following into thinking he was going one way, when he intended to go another.

But who would be following him? He probably thought Simon was dead. He hadn't bothered to fire a second shot or to make sure his quarry was mortally injured—he had been too intent on kidnapping Andi and leaving. That was a mistake Simon would make sure he paid for.

He slowed for the light at the turnoff to Fairplay. Which direction had Victor traveled? If he was working with Metwater, he might have headed back to Denver to meet up with the Prophet. Even if he wasn't working with Metwater, Denver offered more places to hide and more opportunities to move on to other cities, states or countries.

The light turned green and Simon accelerated forward. He had no idea how much time had passed between the shooting and when he had recovered his senses, but it couldn't be very long. Then he had to include the time he had spent changing the tire. Whatever that added up to, Victor had a good head start. Simon was tempted to use his lights and siren to pass the few vehicles on the road, but he didn't want to give Victor warning that he was following. Better to run silent and travel as fast as he dared.

Which wasn't that fast, considering the road was still coated with ice in places. He passed through the desolate stretch of country where he and Andi had almost been stranded yesterday. The wind had whipped the snow into waves in the empty fields, and ice glinted on the barbed wire fencing. A coyote trotted across the highway ahead, disappearing in the clumps of trees along a creek.

Red brake lights glowed ahead and Simon slowed, then stopped. He was last in a line of about eight vehicles, with no oncoming traffic. Frustrated by the delay, he turned on his flashers and pulled into the opposing lane and made his way to the head of the line. He stared into each vehicle he passed, but none of them held a blond Russian or a beautiful pregnant woman.

At the head of the line, a Park County Sheriff's deputy had his cruiser positioned across both lanes, blocking traffic. Just past him, a jackknifed semi truck lay on its side at the bottom of the pass. Simon stopped his cruiser and got out. The deputy—not the one who had helped Simon the day before—nodded in greeting. "When did this happen?" Simon asked.

"About five minutes ago," the deputy said. "Fortunately, nobody's hurt. Driver got out okay." He nodded to the side of the road, where a man in a shearling-lined denim jacket stood, hands in pockets, frowning at the disabled truck.

Simon looked beyond the truck, to the empty northbound lane. If Victor had come this way, he was out of Simon's reach now. "Looks like you've got everything under control," he said.

"Just waiting on the wrecker, but it will be a while," the deputy said. "They said they have to get someone from Denver. If I were you, I'd try another route."

"Thanks, I'll do that." He returned to his cruiser, drove past the growing line of waiting traffic, then pulled over to the shoulder and took out his phone.

Sergeant Daley answered promptly. "What's up, Woolridge?" he asked. "But before you ask—no, we haven't found Metwater yet. He's gone off the radar."

"I've got a different problem now. A guy who may or may not be working with Metwater—a Russian who goes by the name Victor Krayev—has kidnapped Andi—Ms. Daniels." He gave Daley the descriptions of both Andi and Victor.

"We'll put out an APB," Daley said. "Got a description of a vehicle they might be traveling in?"

"Unfortunately, no. I never got a good look."

"Got the jump on you, did he?"

"He shot me. Knocked the wind out of me, but my vest did its job."

"Ouch. Knew a guy that happened to—he ended up with a bruised liver. But considering the alternative…"

"Yeah," Simon said. "I think my guy is headed for Denver, but I don't know for sure. I'm stuck in Fairplay, with the road closed. I'm

going to try going around through Breckenridge, but it will take longer."

"Don't bother," Daley said. "Interstate 70 is
shut down too. Better to hunker down and wait
out the weather. I'll let you know if we get any
leads."

"Thanks." He ended the call, then immediately phoned Ranger Headquarters.

Randall Knightbridge answered. "Hey,
Simon! We thought maybe you'd decided to
run off to Bermuda or something."

"Bermuda would be nice, considering the
weather here," he said, frowning at the lower-
ing clouds that promised more snow.

"Nice and sunny here," Randall said. "But
I hear the other side of the Divide is getting
hammered."

"Is the commander in? I need to speak to
him."

"Hang on a sec."

A moment later Graham picked up the phone. "What's the latest?" he asked.

Simon gave him as brief a report as he dared. "Are you all right?" Graham asked.

"I'm fine." He rubbed his chest, which was bruised and sore, but nothing a couple of aspirin and a good night's sleep wouldn't help. "I don't know about Andi. I don't know what Victor wants with her. And I'm stuck here with the roads closed and more snow coming."

"You don't know for sure he went to Denver," Graham said. "And while we can't rule out that he might be working with Metwater, we have nothing that tells us he is. So where else could he have gone?"

"Anywhere." Simon looked around him at the empty landscape. Two-lane dirt tracks led off from the paved road to remote ranches and national forest land. Maybe Victor had a hideout somewhere along one of those roads.

"Where did he think you were headed?" Graham asked.

"I've been telling people we were going to Breckenridge. I thought it would throw him off track."

"Then it's possible he headed there. Maybe because he thinks Metwater will be there too."

"Maybe." Simon shifted the car into gear. "One thing, at least—I can get to Breck from here. I'm going to check it out." And hope he wasn't already too late.

Chapter Thirteen

Though Andi kept her body still, her mind raced as they left Fairplay behind and climbed above tree line on the icy two-lane road. All color seemed bleached from the landscape of white snow, gray sky and black asphalt. The desolate country drove home how alone she was now. If she was going to survive, she had to come up with a plan on her own. She couldn't count on help from anyone else.

She glanced at the man in the driver's seat. Victor was young, good-looking and confident, like so many men she had known. Daniel had certainly fit that mold, but as much as his looks and confidence had drawn her in, she knew he had underestimated her. He'd mistaken her calm for passivity, her gentleness for weakness. Victor had made the same mistake. He hadn't bothered to tie her up because, hey, what was a pregnant woman going to do to him? Especially when he was holding a gun on her. She couldn't fight him in her condition, and it wasn't as if she was going to run away.

Not only did men like Victor and Daniel see her as weak, they saw her as disposable. Interchangeable. They would use her as long as it suited their purpose, then put her aside—or worse. She didn't trust her chances with either one of them now. She couldn't forget the feel of that knife Daniel had held to her throat.

Traffic slowed as they approached the small community of Alma, with its clusters of vacation cabins and false-fronted stores along the highway. "Some tourist afraid to drive on ice,"

Victor muttered as they joined a line of cars crawling through town. He pounded the steering wheel. "Pull over and park, you idiot!" he said.

Focused as he was on the cars ahead, he wasn't looking at Andi. He probably wasn't even thinking about her. She reached around and carefully undid her seat belt, holding it in place with her left hand so that he wouldn't notice it was loose. With her right hand, she thumbed the lock open and gripped the door release. The car rolled to a stop and she said a quick prayer, then shoved open the door and stumbled out.

Victor's shout pursued her as she shuffled across the snow toward the first building she saw—a log cabin on the side of the road, children's toys scattered across the snowy front yard. Brakes squealed and more shouts rose, but she ignored them and pounded on the door. "Please let me in!" she pleaded. "I need help!"

The door opened and a short woman with a mass of curly red hair answered. "I need to call the police," Andi said. "Please help me." She was crying now, her nose running, her hair falling in her eyes.

"What's going on?" A man appeared behind the woman—a very tall, very broad man with a long black beard down to the middle of his chest.

"Call the police," Andi said. "A man is trying to kidnap me."

"My wife and I were just having a little fight." Victor's hand closed around Andi's upper arm, pulling her away from the door.

Andi turned to look at Victor. He was smiling, but his eyes flashed with violence. He had driven the car halfway into the yard of the cabin. It sat now, both doors open, engine running. "No!" she protested, and tried to pull away.

"She's moody because of the baby," Victor said, and yanked harder on her arm.

"Let her go."

The big bear of a man stepped in front of Victor, glaring at him. "Let her go and leave. She doesn't want to go with you."

Victor stared up at him. Andi wondered if he would pull out his gun and shoot the man, the way he had shot Simon. Had she made a mistake, involving innocent people in her troubles?

"I'm calling the police." The woman behind the man held up a cell phone, then punched in three numbers—Andi assumed nine-one-one.

"All right, I'm leaving." Victor released her and backed away, hands in the air. "Andi, when you've calmed down, you know how to reach me," he said.

The bearded man might have been able to tackle and hold Victor, but Andi didn't want to risk the gun making an appearance, so she said nothing and let him leave. The woman put her arm around Andi's shoulder. "Come inside and get warm. The sheriff is sending someone over."

"Thank you," Andi said, her voice catching. "Thank you so much."

"I got his license plate number," the bearded man said. He nodded to Andi. "Did he hurt you?"

"No...only frightened me." She hugged herself, pulling the coat more tightly around her, but was still unable to get warm.

"You're shaking," the woman said. She led Andi to a sofa near a glowing wood stove. "Sit down here. I was heating up some soup for our lunch. Would you like some? And maybe a cup of hot tea?"

"Yes, that would be wonderful." Andi sat, hoping the shaking would subside soon.

"I'll get the soup and tea," the man said. "You stay here with her." He left the room, his slippers making a shuffling noise on the wood floor.

The woman sat beside Andi and began rubbing her back. "I'm Carrie, and my husband is Lyle," she said.

"I'm Andi."

"Are you okay?" Carrie asked. "Is the baby okay?"

Would she ever really be okay again? Simon was dead, she'd been betrayed by Daniel, her father was in prison and her baby's father was dead...she shook her head. "I'm fine. I'm just...a little overwhelmed."

Carrie glanced back toward the door. "Was that your husband? Or boyfriend?"

Andi shook her head. "It's a long story, but he isn't either of those things."

Lyle returned, carrying a tray with a bowl of soup, a spoon and napkin and a mug with a tea bag floating in hot water. Andi looked at the food and tears came to her eyes—not because she was so hungry and it looked so good, though both of those things were true, but because it represented so much kindness from two strangers.

Pull yourself together, she told herself. *You have to stay strong.*

"Thank you so much," she said again, and accepted the bowl of soup Carrie handed her.

"Don't let me keep you from your own lunch," she said.

"It can wait." Lyle settled into a worn brown leather recliner across from her and continued to study her. "You're not from around here, are you?"

She shook her head and sipped the soup—vegetable, and not from a can. Delicious. "I'm from near Montrose." That was as close to a home as she had had in a while.

A knock on the door interrupted them. Carrie left to answer it and returned a moment later with a Park County Sheriff's deputy. "This is Andi, and she's the reason I called," Carrie said. "A man was trying to make her go with him and she didn't want to go."

The officer came to stand in front of Andi. "Deputy Paul Chasen," he said, handing her a card. "Tell me what happened."

Andi set aside the half-finished bowl of soup, picked up the cup of tea and sipped it cautiously. It smelled of cinnamon and apples and tasted of honey. "My name is Andi Matheson," she said. "I was traveling to Montrose with Agent Simon Woolridge, a member of the Ranger Brigade, operating out of Black

Canyon of the Gunnison National Park. Our car had a flat and when Simon—Agent Woolridge—got out to look at it, a man I know only as Victor drove up, shot Simon in the chest, pulled me out of the car and took me with him."

"That's the man you ran away from?" Lyle asked. "A guy who shot a cop?"

"Where did this shooting occur, and when?" Deputy Chasen asked.

"Less than half an hour ago, just outside of Fairplay, on Highway 285." She swallowed another knot of tears. "I'm sure the cruiser is still there. And Simon's body."

Chasen pulled out his phone and relayed this information to someone on the other end, watching Andi carefully the whole time. When he was done, he pocketed the phone once more. "There is no vehicle on the side of the road, and no body," he said. "Why don't you try again—and with the truth this time."

"Everything I said is true!" Andi protested. "There was a shot, Simon slumped to the ground, then Victor dragged me away and said he was taking me to Breckenridge. When we came through town another car was holding up traffic. We rolled to a stop, I bailed out of the car and came here for help."

"I have the license plate number for the car the guy was driving," Lyle said. "And he was being rough with her, trying to drag her away."

"Give me the number." Chasen called it in. This time when he hung up, he looked less severe. "The car was stolen from a guy in Fairplay this morning," he said. "But we still haven't had any report of a body. That's a busy stretch of highway, even in this weather. Somebody would have reported it by now."

"I don't understand," Andi said. "I saw him

fall. There was a hole in his chest." She swallowed hard, fighting nausea as she relived the horror of that moment.

"Is there anyone else who can confirm your story?" he asked.

"The Ranger Brigade can confirm part of it," she said.

It took a few minutes, but the deputy was able to get a number for the Ranger Brigade from information and made the call. "I've got a woman named Andi Matheson here who claims she was kidnapped by someone named Victor, who killed one of your guys, Simon Woolridge."

He listened a moment, then held out the phone for Andi. "He wants to talk to you."

"Andi?" The voice was one she recognized as belonging to the Ranger Brigade commander.

"He killed Simon," she said. "I saw it happen. I'm so sorry." Then the tears she had been holding back for so long refused to be kept inside any longer. She sobbed into the phone, the pain too much to bear.

"Andi, listen to me!" The commander's voice was kind, but firm. "Simon isn't dead!"

She sniffed, and Carrie stuffed tissues into her hand. Andi dabbed at her nose. "Why do you say that?" she asked. "I saw him fall."

"He was wearing a bulletproof vest," the commander said. "It's part of the uniform. The impact knocked the breath out of him. He called just a little while ago and told me everything. He's all right, and he's looking for you."

Tears flowed again, but this time they were tears of relief. "Tell him I'm right here, waiting," she said.

SIMON HAD ALMOST reached the little town of Alma when he got the call about Andi. Five minutes later, he was standing on the doorstep of the house where she had sought refuge. The bearded man who answered the door sized him up, gaze lingering on the hole in the breast of Simon's coat. He stepped back and motioned behind him. "She's in here," he said.

Andi tried to stand to greet him, but almost lost her balance. A short, redheaded woman put her arm around her and urged her to sit back down. She sat, but reached up to Simon, tears streaming down her face. His throat tightened as her arms came around him. "I'm okay," he said, patting her back. "I'm okay."

She wouldn't release her hold on him, so he ended up seated on the sofa next to her. A sheriff's deputy approached. "Paul Chasen," he said, offering his hand.

"Simon Woolridge." The two men shook. "The guy you're looking for was driving a car he jacked in Fairplay this morning," Chasen said. "My guess is he'll ditch it at the first opportunity and steal another. But he'll probably have to wait until he gets to Breckenridge to do it. There's not much between here and there."

Simon nodded. His first instinct was to take off after Victor, but Andi was his priority now. "I need to get Andi to Montrose," he said. Until she was safe, he couldn't leave her.

"She needs somewhere quiet and away from this stress." The redheaded woman who sat on the other side of Andi spoke. "She could have this baby any minute now, and she shouldn't be chasing lunatics all over the country."

"We've got a safe place waiting for her," Simon said. He removed Andi's arm from around him, though he continued to hold her hand. "Are you ready to go?" he asked.

"I just need to use the ladies' room," she said.

"I'll pack some food for the road," the redhead said. "It's a long way to Montrose."

"The weather isn't looking too good," Chasen said. "You'd better get going before Monarch Pass gets socked in. From there you should be okay. The roads on the other side of the divide are still reporting clear."

"This weather has been chasing us the whole trip," Simon said.

He stood. Chasen studied the tear in Simon's coat. "You really took a direct hit and got away unhurt?" he asked.

"Knocked the wind out of me," Simon said. "A few bruises." He fingered the hole in his jacket. "I'll need a new coat. And I guess a new vest."

Chasen shook his head. "They tell you about stuff like that in training, but you always wonder."

Andi returned to the room, the redhead right behind her. She handed Simon a shopping bag. "There's water and juice and some sandwiches and stuff in there." She looked at Andi. "I remember with my two, I was always hungry."

"Thank you." Andi hugged the woman, and then the bearded man, and shook hands with Chasen. "Thank you so much for everything," she said.

"Yes. Thanks," Simon echoed. "I don't want to think about what might have happened if you had refused to help Andi."

"We never would have turned her away," the woman said. "You two take care."

They set out again. Neither of them said anything for a while.

"I'm glad you're okay," Simon said finally.

"I'm so relieved you weren't hurt," Andi said at the same moment.

He glanced at her and she smiled. He returned the grin. "Nothing like coming back from the dead to give a man a new perspective," he said. Then he sobered. "I'm sorry I couldn't keep Victor from getting to you."

"If you hadn't been knocked senseless, he might have realized you were still alive and shot you in the head," she said. "I'm just glad I got away."

"How did you get away?" he asked. "No one ever said."

"I waited until the car slowed to almost a stop, then I unlocked the door, opened it and got out. He hadn't bothered to tie me up or anything because, hey, what was a pregnant woman going to do?"

"He might have shot you." A shiver ran through him at the thought.

"I thought about that, but he was focused on driving. I just hoped that if I was quick enough, he wouldn't have time to fire, not without losing control of the car."

"You took a big risk," Simon said.

"I had to get away from him. There was something in his eyes that was just so cold." She rubbed her arms, as if warding off a chill.

"Did he say what he was going to do to you?" Simon asked. "Why he wanted you?"

"He wanted to use me as bait to get to Daniel." She shifted toward him, her voice rising with indignation. "He thought I was the Prophet's great love or something, and he said if Daniel wouldn't come to rescue me, he would come for his child." She rubbed her hand across her belly. "I didn't tell him Daniel isn't my baby's father—or that he doesn't care two cents about me anymore."

"So Victor isn't working with Metwater," Simon said.

"No. But he wants to lure Daniel to him. He wants to talk to him about his brother. But he wouldn't say why."

"Word was David Metwater was in deep to

the *Bratva*," Simon said. "Maybe they expect Daniel to pay his brother's debts."

"Maybe so. Victor said Daniel was hiding out in the wilderness, and maybe there was something to that. I know he was afraid of the men who killed his brother—and who can blame him for that?"

"So we know why Victor wanted you, but we still don't know why Metwater is so set on getting you back," Simon said.

"I think I might know." She fingered the locket, feeling the shape of the diamond through the fine knitwork of her sweater. "Victor said Daniel had a key—a safe-deposit box key. Victor asked me if I had the key. I'm pretty sure he said the box it was to contained a million dollars."

"The key in that locket is a safe-deposit box key," Simon said.

"I know." She fished the locket from beneath

her sweater and felt along the side for the catch. The front sprang open and she worked her fingernail underneath the key, which was wedged tightly in the locket's small interior hollow. "There's no bank name on it," she said. "Just a number." She squinted to read it. "Nine, six, two."

"That would be the box number, I'm guessing," Simon said. "I think it's pretty standard not to have any other identifying information on them."

"Would a million dollars fit in a safe-deposit box?" she asked.

"If the money is in large bills," he said. "I think you can rent some fairly large boxes."

"Then why does Daniel need my money if he already has a million stashed away?" she asked.

"If it's a million he—or his brother—stole from the Russian mob, the money is probably too hot for him to touch," Simon said. "And then there's the whole greed angle. If one million is good, three or four are even better."

"To think I almost let him take everything from me," she said. "I can't believe I was so stupid."

"You were trusting," he said. "You wanted to believe in something good. Don't beat yourself up about it."

She took his hand. "Thank you for saying that. I hope I've learned something from this whole experience."

What could he say to that? *You're welcome* was lame, as if he had done some great thing for her. "You were strong enough to risk running away from Victor, where you weren't sure what you had to run to," he said. "Remember that."

She nodded and released his hand. Silence settled around them once more. It wasn't a strained silence, but one of contentment to be with each other without speaking. Snow began to fall more heavily, fat white flakes that clung to the windshield wipers and frosted the road signs. Simon's chest ached, but all he could do was try to ignore it.

They passed through the small towns of Johnson Village and Poncha Springs and made the turn up toward Monarch Pass, but as they approached the bottom of the pass, Simon saw the sign he had been half expecting, but dreading.

"The pass is closed," Andi said, as Simon pulled the cruiser to the shoulder.

He didn't answer, but pulled up a road report on his phone. "Cochetopa Pass is open," he said. "We can go around." The road that direction was narrow and winding, and would add hours to their trip, but he didn't see any alternative.

"Oh, Simon." She imbued those two words with all the frustration and dread he felt. "That will take hours. I don't think I can do it."

"We don't really have any choice," he said. "I need to get you to Montrose, where you'll be safe."

"We do have a choice," she said. "We can turn around and go to my uncle's cabin. It isn't far. We can spend the night there, rest and wait out the weather."

"I don't know,' he said.

"We'll be safe there. We have food. There's a woodstove and you can build a fire." She took his hand again. "All I want is one night in the place where I always felt most at home. One night alone, with you."

He stared at the snow, which looked for all the world as if someone were shaking out the entire contents of a feather bed factory over their heads. He could drive all the way around to Cochetopa Pass, only to find it was closed by then as well. He and Andi were both exhausted, cold, and hurting—the kind of condition in which people made mistakes. His goal was to make sure she was safe, and her uncle's cabin seemed as secure—maybe more so—than any safe house. "All right," he said. "One night."

One night alone together. If nothing else, he knew it was something he would remember for the rest of his life.

Chapter Fourteen

On the drive to the cabin, Andi sat forward in the seat, clutching the dashboard, heart racing with equal parts anticipation and dread. She had lost so much in the past few years that she half expected to find the cabin had been razed, or that the cozy retreat she had so cherished had morphed into a dismal shack.

When the cabin finally came into view, she let out a cry of relief, almost bouncing up and down with joy. "That's it," she said. "Turn in here." The single-story log building was almost hidden in a forest of pine and fir, its steeply pitched metal roof streaked with rust.

The same redwood Adirondack chairs Andi remembered from previous visits flanked the front door, even if the once-cheerful red of the door was now faded to a muted brick.

Simon bumped down the rutted driveway and parked at the bottom of the front steps. Andi popped her seat belt and had the door open before he had even come to a complete stop. "He always kept the key around here," she said, moving around to the side of the cabin, where a massive pine tree stood next to the old-fashioned outhouse. Reaching up, she felt for the nail, and the single key hanging there. Triumphant, she snagged the key and held it aloft.

Simon motioned for her to lead the way up the steps and across the porch. She fitted the key in the lock and pushed open the door. The weak light that filtered through the windows showed a room that served as kitchen, dining and living room, with a three-burner gas stove, a propane refrigerator, sink, square wooden table with four chairs, a sagging couch and armchair and a woodstove set against the back wall.

"That door leads to the bedroom," Andi said, pointing to the open door on the west wall. "And the ladder in the corner goes up to a loft. That's where I always slept. What do you think?"

Simon nodded. "It looks good. We should be all right here."

Not a ringing endorsement, but she would take it. She went to the table and lifted off the chimney of a glass kerosene lantern, turned up the wick and lit it with a match from the box that sat beside the lamp. Two more lamps fit into sconces on the walls. They cast a golden glow that dispelled some of the gloom.

"I should start a fire," Simon said, going over to the stove.

"There's a woodpile around back," Andi said. She bustled around, pulling things out of cabinets, wiping down the table with a rag. Being here energized her. She felt sure of herself here, and safe in a way she couldn't have felt on the road.

Simon left and returned a moment later with an armful of wood. "I'll start the fire, then get our things from the cruiser," he said. "Then I might check in with the Denver cops, see if they have anything new for me." He had called the commander and informed him of their change of plans when they had stopped for gas and a few more groceries on their way back through Johnson Village.

"Unless things have changed, you won't have a cell phone signal here," Andi said.

He scowled, something he did all too often,

she thought. She didn't sense any real anger behind his curmudgeonly expressions though. She thought of them as a kind of habit, or a shield to make other people keep their distance. She had done something similar when she played the role of haughty socialite. That part of her life seemed like years ago now.

"I don't like being out of touch," he said as he arranged kindling inside the woodstove.

"It's only one night." She stood beside him and watched him work. "I know it probably seems strange to you, but I like being where it feels like no one else can reach us."

"As long as you don't decide to go into labor tonight."

She laughed. "I don't think it's a matter of deciding," she said. "But don't worry—I feel great." All the terror and despair from earlier in the day had yielded to a kind of euphoria. Simon was alive. She was alive. They were safe.

And they were together. Whatever they had between them—whatever she sensed was building—seemed too tenuous to last outside the crazy situation they found themselves in, yet her feelings for him overshadowed her doubts. Maybe this caring cop wouldn't want to waste time with her once he had delivered her into someone else's oversight, but right now, with circumstances forcing them together, she was going to hold on to whatever he was willing to give her.

"I think that's going to do it," he said as flames licked up the side of the logs in the stove. He made sure the flue was open, shut the stove door and dusted his hands on his pants. "I'll get the groceries and the luggage."

By the time he returned, she had lit the stove and put a kettle on to boil. "We have tea or instant coffee," she said, studying the supply of staples in the cupboard. "Or the water Carrie sent with us."

"Coffee is fine." He removed his coat and hung it on a peg by the door. Then he un-packed the food while she got out cups and plates. "Your friend Carrie must have thought we were going to Montrose by way of Texas," he said as he surveyed the sandwiches, fruit, chips and cookies in the bags.

"She wanted to make sure we didn't go hun-gry," Andi said. "She seemed like the nurtur-ing type. Good thing too. Not everyone would let a crazed, weeping woman into her home."

"I guess we both have had our share of luck today," he said.

They sat down to lunch with coffee for him and tea for her. The simple food tasted so good, and not merely because of her increased ap-petite. Eating a meal in a place you wanted to be, with someone you wanted to be with, was the best seasoning.

The meal done, Simon pushed his chair back. "You should rest," he said. "I'll have a look around outside so I don't disturb you."

"First, I want to have a look at your chest." She had seen the bullet strike him, had watched him fall. Until she saw his wound—or lack of it—she couldn't quite accept that he was really all right.

"There's nothing to look at," he said.

"How do you know? Have you undressed and examined the wound?"

"There hasn't been time for that."

"There's time now." She pushed back her chair and stood. "There's even a first aid kit in the closet if we need it."

"You're not going to take no for an answer, are you?"

"No, I'm not."

He moved to the sofa and she followed. He removed his gun belt and draped it over the back of the sofa, then unbuttoned his shirt and slid out of it. The Kevlar vest was a bulky, black shield over his torso, the place the bullet had hit barely visible as a small tear in the fabric.

He hesitated a moment, then took off the vest, muscles bunching with the movement. "Oh, Simon," she breathed, when she saw the angry purple bruising across his sternum.

He looked down at himself and winced.

"Does it hurt?" she asked.

"A little."

She brushed her fingertips across his shoulder, then bent and kissed the bruise, the gentlest flutter of her lips that nevertheless made him draw in a sharp breath. "I'm sorry," she said, and tried to move back, but he pulled her to him once more.

"That wasn't a sound of complaint," he said, eyes dark with passion.

The need within her—a different kind of hunger that had lain just beneath the surface all day—surged inside her. She wrapped her arms around him and kissed him, all of her longing and wanting and waiting telegraphed in the meeting of their lips.

"You're the most amazing woman I've ever met," he said, stroking her cheek, as if he needed to touch her to reassure himself she was real.

"Come to bed with me," she urged. "I want you to make love to me."

"I want that too," he said. "But are you sure? With the baby?"

"We may have to make a few…accommodations…for the baby, but you can't hurt it. And I think it would do us both good."

His answer was to kiss her again, the burn of

his day-old beard against her face a reminder that this was no fantasy, but achingly real—and for now, at least, so right.

SIMON FOLLOWED ANDI to the bedroom, where they were confronted by the unmade bed. "There should be linens in the closet," she said, crossing the room to a narrow door. He watched her move, with the careful, heavy walk of the very pregnant. There was still time to stop this—to turn around and walk out of the room and out of the house. He could shovel snow or chop wood or find some way to work off his lust.

But then she turned and smiled at him—as if he was the only man she had ever wanted, and he knew he wouldn't leave unless she ordered him away. He reached to take the stack of sheets from her, and his fingertips brushed the underside of her breast. It was as if she had a direct connection to his groin, pulling the tension there tighter.

They made the bed together, then she turned her back to him and began to undress. He watched, mesmerized, as she stripped, revealing full, heavy breasts and the taut, rounded mound of her abdomen. She was so obviously, intensely female and his every response felt heightened.

She looked over her shoulder at him. "Well?" she said, with a pointed look at his trousers.

He stripped quickly, leaving his clothes where they fell on the floor, and moved in behind her, caressing her curves, kissing the soft roundness of her shoulder and the satiny skin of her throat, holding the weight of her breasts in his hands and wishing, not for the first time, that he had had a part in making the child inside her.

She cupped his face in her hands and kissed

him fiercely, eyes dark with need, breathing rapid. "I don't want to wait anymore," she said.

"No," he agreed.

She knelt on the bed and he positioned himself behind her, hands cradling her hips, her rounded belly. "Hey, what's this?" he asked, running his thumb over the tattoo of a pink rosebud on the curve of her bottom.

She looked back at him and grinned. "That's my little secret."

"Mine now too," he said. He moved his hands around to the front, massaging her breasts.

"Yes, that feels so good," she said. She closed her eyes and arched her back. "Yes."

She was ready for him, and he eased into her slowly, alert to any sign of resistance. There was none, and when she tightened around him he went a little senseless. He cradled her in his arms, wrapped over her and around her and in her. When he moved his hand lower to fondle her, she moaned and thrust back hard against him, her uninhibited passion fueling his own desire. But he held himself back, focusing on her, on teasing and pleasing her, drawing out her pleasure as well as his own.

She moved easily beneath him, setting the pace, thrusting back against him, then rocking forward, eyes closed, a half smile curving her lips as she lost herself in some private pleasure. Watching her fueled his own arousal, and he indulged himself in the pleasure of exploring her body, running his hands over her breasts, tracing the curve of her back with his lips. The tension building in her moved into his body as well, until he was holding his breath, balanced on the edge of his own release, waiting for her.

She came with a loud cry, convulsing in his arms, the intensity of the moment stripping him of the last of his control and he followed her over the edge, rocking against her until he was spent and breathless, every pain and doubt and coherent thought momentarily banished.

Afterward they slept, the sated, cocooned sleep of those who had found safe harbor in each other's arms. When Simon woke it was almost dark, only a thin gray light coming through the windows. He eased out of bed and, still naked, went to build up the fire, which had burned down to coals. He found another blanket in the closet and draped it over Andi's sleeping form, then carried his clothes into the living room and dressed.

Outside, the snow had stopped falling, though a thick white blanket lay over the landscape, softening hard edges and hiding details of the world outdoors. Simon walked around the house, assessing its defensive position. Not that he expected to have to hold off intruders, but his training was too ingrained to ignore.

He shoveled a path to the outhouse, then decided to park the cruiser out of sight, around the back of the house. The smoke from the stovepipe and lights in the windows made it evident the cabin was occupied, but he didn't have to advertise by whom. On his way back up to the house he met Andi, on her way back from the outhouse. "Going somewhere?" she asked.

"Not without you." He gathered her close. "How about some supper?"

"You really know the way to my heart."

They decided to eat in front of the fire. He insisted she sit on the sofa while he heated soup and served it on a tray. She sighed. "This is so nice," she said.

"Yeah, it is." It couldn't last—she was still in danger, and he still needed to get her to a safe house and set to work finding and stopping not only Daniel Metwater, but Victor Krayev. But he would try to set that aside for a few more hours, and focus on enjoying this night with her.

"Tell me about the rosebud," he said. "How did you end up with a tattoo on your backside?"

She laughed. "I got it on a dare. Silly, I guess, but it made me feel rebellious and brave. I know to everyone else it looked like I had the perfect life—looks, money and social prestige. But the one thing I didn't have was freedom. Someone was always watching me—either my father, to make sure I wasn't doing anything to tarnish his reputation, or the bodyguards he hired to protect me, or the press who reported on our every move."

"So you got a tattoo."

She laughed again—a lilting cascade of notes that did crazy things to his insides. "I know, right? No drugs, sex or rock and roll for me. I got a tattoo of a flower where most people will never see it." She shrugged. "I was a good kid, I guess. But in the end, I could never be good enough. I could never live up to my dad's idea of what I should be."

"I know what that's like," he said.

She put a comforting hand on his knee. "Did your father expect you to be a police officer like him? Surely he would be proud of you now."

"I'll never be the cop he was," Simon said. He could never be as genuinely *good* as his father—and his mother and uncles and aunts—had been. They had all devoted their lives to serving others. Simon had been cut from a different mold. He had realized it when he was still young, and he was sure everyone else could see it. He had come from a family of saints, and he was the bad apple of the bunch.

"You're the best cop I've ever known." She squeezed his knee and leaned toward him, her tone teasing. "At least you don't have any tattoos, do you? Or did I miss something?"

He shook his head. "No tattoos."

"Why not?" she asked. "You don't believe in them?"

"I like being different."

"You like being contrary." She nodded.

"All right, that too."

"At least you didn't get one and then regret it," she said. "I know people who have done that."

"So do I." He yawned. The warm fire and easy company had relaxed him completely. Andi was right—they had both needed this break from the constant stress of the past few days.

"Daniel had a tattoo he was ashamed of," she said. "He almost always kept it covered."

All lethargy vanished at this revelation. He looked at her intently. "I saw him dancing around the fire in little more than a loincloth," he said. "I don't remember any tattoo."

"It was on his biceps." She indicated a spot on the outside of her left arm. "A lion with devil horns, mouth open in a roar, blood dripping from its fangs." She shuddered. "Pretty gruesome. He told me he hated it, and wished he had never gotten it."

Simon and his fellow Rangers had been studying Daniel Metwater intently for months, but he was sure none of them knew anything about a tattoo. "How do you cover up something like that?" he asked. "Makeup?"

She shook her head. "He had this elastic sleeve. It was flesh colored and really thin, but opaque. He could pull it on like an armband. You could hardly see it. For the bonfires, he would wear these tribal armbands over it and no one could tell. I probably would never have known about it if I hadn't walked in on him getting dressed one night, before he put on the sleeve."

"How did he react when you saw it?" Simon asked.

"He was angry, but then he calmed down and apologized. He said he was just so ashamed of the ink—that he didn't think it set a good example for his followers. He asked me to promise to never say anything about it to anyone." She made a face. "I guess I just broke that promise."

"When a guy puts a knife to your throat and threatens to kill you, I think it negates any promises you made to him," Simon said.

"I guess so." She shifted to stare into the fire, seemingly lost in thought. Was she thinking of Daniel Metwater, trying to reconcile her love for him with all he had done to her? A black mood settled over Simon at the thought. She deserved so much better than Metwater, but when had love ever had anything to do with merit?

"I've been thinking a lot lately about all the things I could have done differently in my life." She let out a heavy sigh. "I guess the prospect of being a mother has me reassessing everything, but especially my bad choices."

"You trusted people who betrayed you," Simon said. "Beating yourself up over that won't do any good."

"Oh, I know that." She turned to him, her eyes clear and calm. "But I want to make better choices in the future. And I want to do what I can to make up for past mistakes." She took his hand, her grip warm and firm. "Were you serious when you said you could help me get in touch with my dad?"

"If that's what you want, yes."

"I don't know what I want. But…he's the only family I have. And I miss him." She shook her head. "I don't miss the man he was the last few years—driven by ambition and greed—but the father he was when I was younger, before my mother died. What he did—killing Frank— was horrible. But I think, in a twisted kind of way, he believed he was protecting me."

"You could write to him," Simon said. "Then if that goes okay, you could arrange to visit him—though seeing him in prison will be tough. Emotionally, I mean."

She nodded. "A letter would be a good start. Maybe writing down how I feel about every- thing that has happened would be good for both of us."

He studied the soft curve of her cheek, the silky fall of her hair—she looked impossibly young and innocent, yet she had already seen enough tragedy for a lifetime, and it hadn't broken her. "You're amazing," he said.

She blinked. "Why do you say that?"

"Because you've been through so much, and you're still so good."

She laughed. "There are plenty of people out there who wouldn't agree with you on that."

"I don't care what they think."

Something flared in her eyes—passion or joy—and she leaned forward and kissed him gently on the cheek. "Then I don't care, either."

He pulled her close, and the moment might have evolved into another round of lovemaking, if she hadn't had to stifle a yawn. "Sorry. I don't know why I'm so sleepy."

"I think we're both still catching up from the past few days," Simon said. He stood and offered her a hand. "Come on. Let's go to bed. Tomorrow will be another full day." He hoped it was the day the Rangers captured Daniel Metwater and Victor.

She wrapped her arms around him and

kissed him on the lips. "You're too good to me," she said.

"I'm not that good," he said. Though she certainly made him want to be better.

She smiled and took his hand. "I'll be the judge of that, Officer."

ANDI WOKE WHILE it was still dark, the room cold, though she was warm under the heavy quilts. Her heart pounded, as if she had been running—or awakened in the middle of a nightmare. What had her feeling so panicked? She couldn't remember.

She reached out a hand and felt Simon's solid, warm bulk at her side. Reassurance filled her, and she snuggled back down under the covers and closed her eyes.

Thump! She opened her eyes, heart racing once more. What was that sound?

Creeeak. She tried to tell herself the noise

was merely the old cabin settling, but instinct told her otherwise. It was as if the air around her had shifted—she was sure there was some-one else in the cabin.

"Simon!" She put her mouth next to his ear, her whisper urgent. "Wake up!"

"Mmm." He rolled over and reached for her.

She pushed against his chest. "Wake up! Someone is in the cabin."

He lay still, tensed. There was a sound like something scraping against the floor. Simon sat, pushing back the covers. He took his gun from the nightstand. "Stay here," he said. Then he slipped out of the room.

Chapter Fifteen

Simon eased the door to the bedroom shut behind him, careful not to make a sound. Then he stood still for several minutes, forcing his breathing to slow.

And he listened. His ears strained to hear anything other than the pounding of his own heart.

Scrape. The sound of something being dragged across the floor—not in the cabin itself, but outside, on the front porch. It was a sound effect out of a horror movie, and all the more chilling in real life. Slowly, carefully placing each step, Simon moved toward the front window.

Moonlight illuminated a black-and-white world of snow and shadows. Far to the right of the cabin, in the darkness cast by the building itself, a vehicle hunched—an SUV of some sort, tall and boxy. Footsteps clearly showed in the snow, leading from the vehicle and up the front steps to disappear in the deeper shadows of the porch.

The scraping noise came again—someone prying at the front window, just on the other side of where Simon stood. He moved to the door, hand on the knob. Opening it would probably make enough racket to announce his presence—though he could still likely catch whoever was out there off guard. If the cabin had a back door, he might try to go out that way and sneak up behind the person on the porch, but the only way out the back was through the bedroom window.

The scraping continued, followed by a grunt and a wrenching sound as the intruder succeeded in forcing up the window. Time for Simon to make his move. He started to step forward, when a second shadow emerged from the trees at the edge of the driveway. It skirted past the front of the house without stopping, moving swiftly behind the building and out of sight. The figure at the window gave no indication that he had noticed the newcomer. Was this an accomplice, heading around to cover the back of the house?

This definitely complicated things. It was two against one now, and too much distance separated the intruders for Simon to take them both out at once. He would have to eliminate them one at a time. And he'd need to move quickly.

He eased open the front door and stepped out onto the porch. "Freeze!" he shouted, aiming both his gun and his flashlight at the shadowy figure.

Daniel Metwater squinted into the light, one hand to his eyes to shield them. He fired the pistol he carried in his other hand, the bullets tearing into the wood of the door frame as Simon dove for cover behind the firewood stacked at the end of the porch.

ANDI HUDDLED IN BED, covers pulled tightly around her, as the sharp report of bullets shattered the midnight silence. She strained her ears, listening for cries, but heard nothing more. Moonlight poured through the window to her left, illuminating the room's sparse contents. Her gaze fixed on the bulletproof vest that hung from the bedpost. She should have insisted that Simon put it on before he left the bedroom.

She should have asked him to give her a gun too, so that she could help defend them. She hated sitting here, helpless.

All this fretting over what she should have done wasn't going to help anyone. She eased out of bed and pulled the fur coat over her gown, then sat on the side of the bed to pull on the boots. Maybe they weren't the most practical footwear for evading bad guys in the wilderness, but they were the only shoes she had with her, and they were warm.

She winced and rubbed at her lower back, trying to ease the cramp that tightened her muscles. The Braxton Hicks contractions she had been experiencing on and off for the last two months had started up again. Another sign her body was getting ready to deliver her baby, the women in camp had assured her.

Wait a while longer, little one, she said silently, sending a message to the infant in her womb. *Mommy isn't ready just yet.*

She stood and tiptoed to the bedroom door. Simon had ordered her to stay put, but she had to find out what was going on.

Another blast of gunfire shook the cabin and she stifled a cry, heart pounding painfully. Frantic, she looked around for anything to use as a weapon. Her mind flashed on the old toolbox her uncle kept under the kitchen sink. There would be something in there— a hammer or a big wrench or something she could use to strike out at an attacker. Something to make her feel less helpless.

She eased the door open farther and prepared to move into the front room as more shots sounded from the front of the house, coupled with the noise of shattering glass behind her. Disoriented, she turned and stared at the broken glass scattered across the bed and the floor. Had someone shot out the window? Then she saw the rock, as big as a man's head, that rested in the middle of the bed.

Right about where she had been sitting only moments before.

A man's head and shoulders appeared in the window, and then Victor hoisted himself up over the sill. Andi turned to flee, but he was on her faster than she would have thought possible, his hands holding her roughly.

"You're not going anywhere," he said, his lips brushing the top of her head. "You're mine now, and this time, I'm not going to let you get away."

FROM BEHIND THE WOODPILE, Simon returned fire, but his shot went wide as Metwater retreated around the corner of the house. Metwater's accomplice would have been alerted by now. Simon thought if he hadn't heard Simon's shout, anyone within a mile would have heard those shots. He hoped Andi had the sense to stay put in the bedroom and not go investigating. He glanced over his shoulder, to make sure no one was moving in behind him, then turned back toward where Metwater had disappeared. "Give up!" he called. "I won't let you leave here alive."

Metwater's answer was another volley of shots into the woodpile, sending chunks of wood flying. Simon crouched there, his face pressed against the rough logs, the smell of pine mingling with the sting of cordite. He cursed his choice of cover. He should have retreated into the cabin, where he would be closer to Andi. As long as Metwater had ammo, it didn't matter if he actually hit Simon or not. All he had to do was keep him pinned here while his accomplice got whatever he was after.

It didn't take a genius to figure out what that might be. Andi was the only thing in the cabin worth having. Now she would pay for Simon's poor judgment.

The best he could hope for was to keep Metwater distracted and look for an opening to get to him. "How did you find us?" he called.

"Asteria used to talk about this cabin," Metwater said, using the name he had given Andi. "She even talked about bringing me here to visit someday. I knew she wouldn't get this close without stopping by."

"Why are you here?" Simon asked. "What do you want?"

"I want Asteria."

"Why?"

"She has something that belongs to me."

"What's that?" Was he talking about the necklace, or the key inside it or something else entirely?

"I'm tired of talking. Send her out and I'll let you go."

"Never." He emphasized his point by aiming where he thought Metwater's head might be and firing.

"He's not the one you need to deal with now." The Russian's accent revealed his identity even before Simon turned to see him step from the side of the house. He had one arm around Andi, who was wrapped in the fur coat, wearing her boots. At least Victor had allowed her to dress before bringing her out in the cold.

In the other hand, Victor held a small pistol, the barrel of it pressed to Andi's temple. "Either of you make a move, I'll kill her," he said. "Now throw out your guns."

"Go ahead and shoot her," Metwater said. "It will save me the trouble."

Andi flinched. Victor pulled her more tightly against him. "Now the question I ask myself is—are you serious, or are you bluffing?" he said. Andi didn't make a sound, though her gaze remained fixed on Simon, pleading, her face paper white in the moonlight, eyes huge and dark.

Sweat slicked Simon's hand as he tightened his grip on his gun.

"Don't even think about it, Officer," Victor barked. "Drop your weapon. Now!"

Simon tossed the gun onto the porch. It bounced on the floorboard, then skidded to rest against one of the posts.

"Your turn." Victor addressed Metwater.

Metwater fired, at the same time Andi brought her foot down hard on Victor's instep, driving the stiletto heel of her boot into the top of his foot. With a roar of rage, he grappled to hold her, but she lunged free.

Simon dove for his gun and came up firing. But Victor had already retreated behind the

SUV. Andi had disappeared—Simon hoped somewhere well out of the range of gunfire. He had taken cover behind a large pine tree, halfway between the cabin and the SUV. He was safe for now, but trapped between his two opponents. He leaned against the tree, trying to catch his breath, the cold seeping through his clothes as he listened for sounds of movement from Metwater or Victor.

It was too quiet. Simon worried one of the men—or both—had left and gone after Andi. He focused on the side of the cabin where Metwater had been, unable to detect any movement in the dim light. Somewhere nearby, an engine roared to life. Lights flared on, and a vehicle pulled from the trees farther up the driveway.

"My car!" Victor shouted. He climbed into the SUV and started the engine. Simon aimed for the vehicle, but he only managed a single shot before Victor sped down the driveway.

The rumble of engines and crunch of tires on gravel and snow faded, leaving a ringing silence. Simon stepped out from behind the tree. "Andi!" he shouted.

"I'm right here." She emerged from behind the outhouse.

Simon ran to her and she fell into his arms. He held her tightly for a long moment, unable to speak.

"What happened?" she asked after a long moment.

"They came in two separate cars. Victor left his parked up by the road—probably with the keys in it so he could make a quick getaway if he had to. Metwater's SUV was in the driveway. He took Victor's car and now Victor has his."

Andi frowned. "Did they come here together?"

"I don't know. I'm beginning to think not." Reluctantly, he released her. "Come on," he said. "We have to get out of here."

"Yes, we need to leave," she responded.

"I don't think they'll come back, but they might," he said.

"I'm not worried about that," Andi said. "We need to leave because I think I'm going into labor."

Simon stopped and stared at her. "Are you sure?"

She rubbed her belly. "I've been having pains for a while now," she said. "Then, just now, my water broke." She opened the coat to reveal her soaked gown. "Ready or not, I think I'm going to have this baby."

Chapter Sixteen

Don't be afraid, Andi told herself as another pain rocked her as soon as she and Simon stepped into the cabin. When he looked at her, she forced a smile. "I'm sure we have plenty of time," she said.

"I'll get the luggage," he said. "You wait here."

As soon as he was out of sight, she steadied herself with one hand on the back of a chair. Should she insist they stay here in the cabin, with the fire and bed and shelter? Did cops know anything about delivering babies? Was that part of their training?

But the thought of having her baby out here

all alone terrified her. She wanted doctors and nurses and bright lights, sterile sheets and painkillers if necessary.

Simon emerged from the bedroom, suitcases in hand. He wore his coat now, and when she hugged him, she felt the reassuring hardness of the bulletproof vest. "I'll bring the cruiser around," he said. "You wait here."

Waiting. It seemed that was all she had been doing lately. She leaned back against the porch post and closed her eyes. Had it really only been eight months ago that she had discovered she was pregnant? At the time, she had been nervous but happy, looking forward to building a family with the man she loved— of making a new life of her own that wasn't dependent on her father's wealth or his plans for her future.

But her lover hadn't been so happy, and she had been horrified to learn that he was married, with two other children she had had no idea existed. Her father had been equally unsupportive, offering to pay for an abortion, more concerned with keeping the scandal a secret than worrying about his daughter's feelings.

So she had run away. She hadn't called it that, of course. She had been "moving on" and "striking out on her own," but all she had done was retreat into the wilderness, change her name and become involved with a handsome, charismatic man who was as false as all the other men she had met in her life.

"Lean on me." Simon's arm encircled her and she opened her eyes and looked into his weary, concerned face. She saw strength in his eyes, not scorn or impatience or any of the other emotions she had too often seen in other men's eyes. "Watch your step," he said. "It's icy."

"Bet you're glad I wore these silly boots now," she said as he helped her to the car.

He squeezed her arms. "Don't ever let anyone tell you you don't have guts," he said.

He shut the passenger door, then returned to the cabin to retrieve the bags and load them in the back. Seconds later, he was guiding the cruiser down the snowy driveway.

"Where are we going?" she asked. "I have no idea where the nearest hospital is."

"It's probably in Breckenridge," Simon said. "But all we need is to get back in cell phone range, and we can call for an ambulance."

"Good." She spoke through clenched teeth as another burst of pain rocked through her.

Simon reached over and took her hand. "You okay?" he asked.

She nodded. "I'll be fine. Just...let's get out of here."

He hunched over the steering wheel, gaze

shifting back and forth, searching, she realized, for any sign of Daniel or Victor. "You don't think they're waiting for us, do you?" she asked, anxiously searching the woods closing in on both sides of the road.

"Their tire tracks are headed the same direction we are." Simon indicated the crisp tire tread imprints in the snow on the road. "I think Victor is chasing Metwater."

"I think Victor would have killed me and not thought twice about it," she said. "Daniel wouldn't have cared, either. I'm nothing to them." The knowledge sent a wave of nausea through her.

"They don't have the capacity to care about anyone but themselves," Simon said.

She wanted to ask him if he cared, if he would ever abandon her that way, but the words stuck in her throat. Protecting her was his job, one he was good at. He had admitted he had feelings for her, but clearly duty came first to him. How could she ever fit into his rigid, law-and-order world?

Another pain hit and she was unable to stifle a cry. The car swerved, then righted once more. "Are you all right?" Simon asked.

"Stop asking me that! I don't know if I'm all right. I'm having a baby."

"How far apart are the pains?"

"I don't know."

He glanced at the clock on the dash. "Tell me when the next one hits."

"Okay." She scooted to the edge of the seat, the safety belt straining across her torso, and they both waited in tense silence. She gripped the dash as another pain tore at her. "Now," she gasped.

The lines between Simon's eyes deepened. "About four minutes," he said. He pulled out his phone and frowned at the screen.

"Do you have a signal?" she asked, fighting a wave of panic. What if they didn't make it in time?

He shook his head. "But we'll be in range soon. We'll get an ambulance."

She closed her eyes and clenched her teeth, every sense focused on her body, on the tension and the pain and the child shifting inside her. This was really happening. And she wasn't ready.

The sound of the tires changed as they turned onto pavement, and she opened her eyes again. The highway stretched out in front of them, empty and snow covered, wind stirring up eddies of snow that rose and swirled at headlight level like dancing ghosts.

Simon pulled to the shoulder of the road and took out his phone. "This is Agent Simon Woolridge with the Ranger Brigade, and I'm on highway 285 south of Fairplay," he said.

"The woman with me is in labor. Her pains are four minutes apart."

Andi couldn't hear the voice on the other end of the line. She closed her eyes again and pressed her forehead to the passenger window, the iciness of the glass sending a shiver through her. Wind rocked the vehicle as Simon waited for someone on the other end of the line.

"We're at mile marker… I can't see a mile marker," he said. "But we're just past the turn-off for County Road Twenty-Four… Yes, her water has broken… Yes… No… How long do you think it will be?… No… I'll call you back if I need to."

He ended the call and tossed the phone onto the console, his mouth twisted in an expression of frustration. "What did they say?" Andi asked. "Are they sending an ambulance?"

"They said it will be forty minutes, maybe

an hour," he said. "A major pileup on I-70 has diverted all the local transport, and it will be that long before they can get to us."

She fought down a wave of panic as a hard gust of wind rocked the vehicle. "What were all those questions that you were answering yes and no to?"

He kneaded the bridge of his nose. "They asked if I had ever delivered a baby before."

"Have you?"

"Not exactly." He opened the driver's door and put one foot out. "I'm going to get the first aid kit and some blankets from the back of the cruiser," he said. "I think you should move into the back seat, where you'll have more room."

"What do you mean, not exactly?" she called after him, but he had already shut the door and was walking around to the back of the cruiser.

Icy wind whipped through the vehicle when he opened up the back hatch. Andi turned away from him, wanting to insist that he keep driving—all the way to Breckenridge if he had to. But she knew they didn't have time. The increasingly urgent need to push told her this baby was going to be born, whether she was ready or not.

Simon came around to the passenger side and opened the door, his arms full of blankets. "I'll spread one of these on the seat for you to lie on," he said. "I've got a couple of clean towels, too, and some bottled water."

He reached to help her out and she gripped his hand. "Have you ever delivered a baby?" she asked again, staring hard until he met her gaze.

Before he could answer, another contraction rocked her. She let out a low groan, and Simon massaged her shoulder.

When the pain passed, she let him help her move to the rear seat and scoot back, legs stretched out toward him. A cold wind swirled around the vehicle, hard granules of snow splatting against the open doors and gathering on the floorboards. His eyes met hers once more. If he was afraid, he was doing a good job of hiding it. "I once watched my uncle deliver a baby at a clinic in Mexico," he said. "I was seventeen and I was helping out there for the summer. When they brought the woman in, I think everyone had forgotten I was in the room. I didn't do anything—I stood in the corner and watched."

"What did you think?" she asked.

"I was terrified and fascinated." He made a face. "I remember there was a lot of yelling, and a lot of blood—two things I wasn't used to back then."

"And you are now?"

"Let's just say I've seen more of both over the years. They don't shake me as much now."

"I hope you remember some of what you saw," she said.

He held up a paperback book. "I have some instructions here that should help. But really, there's not a lot I can do. Yours is the hard part."

Another pain rocked her, this one more intense. She tried to stifle her scream by biting her lip, but Simon grabbed her hand and squeezed. "Go ahead and make all the noise you want," he said. "There's no one else out here to hear us anyway."

ANDI'S SCREAMS CUT through Simon like razors. With shaking hands, he tore one of the clean towels into strips, as instructed by the book he had wedged open on the floorboard of the backseat. *Get a grip*, he told himself. *Time to man up and do your job.*

He tried to remember everything his uncle had done when he had delivered that baby in his clinic all those years ago, but he had been so young then, fighting a mixture of horror and embarrassment. There was no room for any of those feelings now.

He glanced up and into Andi's wide, frightened eyes, and tried to force a smile. She was counting on him to get her through this. Her baby was depending on him too. He squeezed her hand. "You're doing great," he said.

"What does the book say?" she asked.

He glanced down at the open pages. "We should see the head at the entrance of the birth canal," he said. "That's called crowning. A couple more strong pushes after that, and the baby will be born. I have to clear any mucous from the baby's mouth and nose and make sure it's breathing, then tie off the cord and keep it warm, and deliver the afterbirth."

"So much to do," she said, before another cry of pain choked off her words.

Following the instructions in the first aid

manual, he laid out a clean towel, water, scissors, first aid tape and alcohol wipes. "Something's happening!" Andi cried.

"I can see the head." Simon dropped to his knees, ignoring the snow and dirt, bracing himself to support the baby when it emerged. He barely registered the crunch of tires on snow, and glanced to his left to see a vehicle pulling in behind him, the grille almost touching the back bumper. Then another cry from Andi forced his attention back to her.

"Another push or two, I think," he said.

"It hurts so much!" she screamed through her tears.

"You can do this." And then he was holding the baby, a writhing, sticky bundle pulsing with life. He stared at it, overwhelmed by such a feeling of awe that he was glad he was already on his knees. The infant was so tiny and perfect, so alive… He shook his head, forcing himself out of his reverie, and consulted the first aid manual. Following the instructions illustrated on the page, he carefully wiped the baby's mouth and nose, then gently turned it over. "It's a girl," he said, surprised at the tears choking his voice.

"Let me see her." Andi struggled to sit up, tears streaming down her face. The baby let out a lusty cry and the sound made Simon laugh. He laid the baby on Andi's stomach, and she spread her hand protectively over the baby's back.

A shadow loomed over him, and something hard pressed against his temple. "How does it feel to bring a new life into the world?" Victor asked. "When you're about to lose yours?"

"GO AWAY!" ANDI SCREAMED. "Don't touch my baby!" Ignoring the pain it cost her, she leaned forward, trying to cover the infant's body with her own.

"I don't care about your brat." Victor kept the gun pressed to Simon's temple, but he was focused on mother and child. "Give me the key."

"The key?" Andi asked.

"Don't be stupid. I know you have the key that belonged to Metwater. Give it to me."

"He hid it in this necklace." She grasped the pendant and tugged, trying to tear it from her neck, but the gold chain refused to budge.

"Give it to me!" Victor roared. Snow swirled around him, collecting in his blond hair and on the shoulders of his wind-whipped coat. He looked like some demon out of a horror novel.

"I'm trying," she cried.

"I need to tie off the umbilical cord," Simon said, his voice eerily calm in the midst of chaos.

"Shut up," Victor said. "If you don't give me the necklace I'll kill him now."

Sobbing, Andi wrenched the necklace free, and hurled it at him. It sailed over Simon's head and landed in the snow. Victor dove for it as Simon rose, his gun drawn, but it was not his bullet that struck Victor in the shoulder and sent him spinning to the side.

Daniel Metwater stepped forward, his foot crunching the necklace into the snow. Victor looked up from where he lay sprawled in the snow, blood dripping from his blasted shoulder, and all the color drained from his face. "You!"

The gun fired again, and red blossomed in the calf of Victor's right leg. His keening wail echoed around them. Andi folded herself more securely over the baby, who cried softly and nestled against her stomach. "I want the key,"

Metwater demanded. "Tell me where it is or I'll shoot again. The other leg this time."

"The necklace," Victor gasped. "The key is in the necklace."

Keeping his eyes and the pistol fixed on Victor, Metwater bent and scooped the necklace from the snow and dropped it in the pocket of his ski jacket. Then he stood over Victor, who bowed his head and buried his face in the snow.

Andi looked away, sure Daniel would kill the Russian now. But instead of the explosion of gunfire, she heard the sound of tearing fabric, as Simon worked to tie off her baby's umbilical cord. "I was paid to kill you once before, David," Victor said. "A fee I was never able to collect."

Metwater leveled the gun at Victor's head. "My name is Daniel. David was my brother."

"No, you're David," Victor said. "You knew

we were closing in on you so you came up with a plan—a smart, perfect plan. You went to your brother Daniel. The good brother who always came through for you, who always got you out of trouble. You invited him to dinner at your place. You drugged him. Then you paid a tattoo artist a lot of money to duplicate your infamous lion tattoo on his arm. Then you shot him and dumped his body in the river, and you stepped into his life. You identified his water-ravaged corpse and arranged for a hasty cremation. With David presumed dead, you didn't have to worry about the *Bratva* coming after you as payback for all the money and drugs you stole from us. But just to be safe, you went into hiding. You became a prophet in the wilderness."

Andi stared at the two men. "That's why you didn't want anyone to see the tattoo," she said.

Metwater's eyes met hers. "You were the

only one who knew," he said. "Once you and your cop friend are dead, I'll be safe."

She clutched at her baby, determined to protect the child. She hadn't come this far to die out here in the snow. "Simon," she whispered.

He glanced up at her and gave a small shake of his head, then reached for the scissors to cut the cord.

"You forgot that the *Bratva* never forgives those who betray them," Victor said. "You were supposed to deliver a million dollars as a favor to us. Instead, you stole the money."

"Lies!" Metwater screamed. "You can't prove any of it."

"I found the tattoo artist," Victor said. "That was a mistake, leaving him alive. Or maybe you did come after him, but too late. He took the money you paid him and ran—it took us quite a while to track him down."

The distant wail of a siren rose over the

whine of the wind. Andi's eyes met Simon's once more. He had risen and was standing between her and the two men. His gun was drawn, but he held it low at his side.

"It's too late for you now," Victor said, his voice strained. "The police are coming for you."

The words were scarcely out of his mouth before Metwater fired again. Andi screamed as the Russian slumped to the ground. Metwater pivoted toward Simon, and Andi screamed again. "No!"

Chapter Seventeen

Simon dropped to a crouch, his hands slippery with the blood of Andi's baby, the gun cold in his hand. Metwater stood with his gun still smoking, calmly taking aim, ready to kill without emotion or regret. He had been cold-blooded enough to kill his own brother, so what were Andi and a cop to him now? He looked on his targets not as adversaries, but prey. He had every tactical advantage over Simon.

Except that Simon was determined to live. He wouldn't leave Andi and her child defenseless. He wouldn't let this killer win.

With a roar of rage, he sprang up and charged

at Metwater, striking him full on, even as a bullet whistled past his head. Metwater landed hard on his back, the gun still in his hand. Simon struck out viciously with a karate chop to Metwater's wrist that sent the gun skittering into a snowbank.

The two men grappled, rolling around on the shoulder of the road, coming to rest against the tires of the ambulance that skidded to a stop beside them. Metwater shoved Simon away from him, scrambled to his feet and lurched to his car. By the time Simon had risen, he was driving away.

Simon searched the snow for his weapon and found it near his cruiser. He wiped it on his jacket and reholstered it, then made his way to where one of the EMTs knelt beside Victor. "He's dead," the EMT said. He stood. "What happened here?"

"It's a long story," Simon said.

"They usually are," the EMT said.

"He's not your patient." Simon led the way to the cruiser and looked in at Andi. She had pulled the fur coat over her and the baby, whom she still cradled on her stomach. She looked pale and frightened.

"Simon!" she said. "I was so afraid."

"Ma'am, let's just have a look here." The two EMTs shouldered Simon aside. While one examined Andi, the other began radioing in particulars, starting with a call for police assistance.

Simon walked to the back of the cruiser and leaned against the bumper, feeling shaky as the adrenaline left him. Cold seeped through his shirt and vest. He should put on his coat, but he was too exhausted to move. Victor's still figure lay a few feet away, facedown in the bloody snow. Wind ruffled his hair and tugged at his jacket.

So Daniel was really David, a man who had killed his own brother, sacrificing the one person he had been closest to, letting him take the fall for the crimes he had committed. He had played the role of the innocent brother for months, and might even have gotten away with it, if not for his own greed. Somehow he had come to the *Bratva*'s attention, and they had figured out his scam.

Andi had seen the damning tattoo, so he had had to come after her. Her millions had been just an added bonus. He might have gotten away long before now, if he hadn't been determined to help himself not only to the stolen million dollars, but to Andi's wealth as well.

Simon turned to stare in the direction Metwater had driven. He was running out of places to hide now. He was getting more desperate, and more reckless. As soon as Simon had Andi settled, he would go after the man who had tried to kill her. He wouldn't stop until he had Metwater in custody.

The EMTs wheeled a gurney across the

snow to the side of the cruiser and transferred Andi and her baby to it. Simon moved around the cruiser to stand beside her. "How are you doing?" he asked. The EMTs had cleaned her and the baby up some, and cut the cord so that she could cradle the now-swaddled newborn to her breast.

"I can't believe what just happened," she said. "Do you think it's true—that Daniel is really David?"

"He didn't deny it," Simon said. He brushed her hair from her eyes, the strands silken against his fingers. "Are you sure you're okay?"

"I'm fine. And the baby is fine—thanks to you. Everything is going to be all right now."

"I forgot to tell you happy birthday earlier," he said.

She gave a weak laugh. "It's been an eventful day." She looked down at the infant at her breast. "I think I already have the best present ever."

"I have some loose ends to tie up here," Simon said. "But I'll be at the hospital to see you as soon as I can."

She nodded and he started to turn away, but she reached out and clutched his hand. "Wait."

He turned back to her. "What is it?"

"They key Daniel—David—was looking for—"

"You did the right thing, giving it up to him. It wasn't worth your life to argue with him."

"No—it wasn't in the necklace. I took it out."

He frowned. "When did you do that?"

"In the cabin. I knew he and probably Victor too, wanted it, and I was afraid of what they would do to me. I thought it would be better if I didn't keep it on me. So I took it out and hid it in the cabin. It's in my uncle's toolbox, under the sink in the kitchen."

"All right. Thanks for letting me know."

"I still can't believe he murdered his own brother," she said. "The brother who had always helped him. His twin. How could anyone do something like that?"

"I don't know. Maybe sometimes something gets broken in a person that makes it easier for them to do horrible things."

"We need to go now," one of the EMTs said. "We need to get mom and baby out of the cold."

Simon hesitated, then bent and kissed Andi, a brief buss on the lips. "I'll be by to see you soon." She would be safe in a hospital, surrounded by other people. He needed to find Metwater, and make sure he didn't come after her again.

"I love you," she said. "Don't ever forget that."

"I love you too. And I won't forget." The words were easier to say than almost anything he had ever said, akin to a miracle, considering how hard and messy he usually found emotions to be. It was as if he had built up a callus over his heart and this beautiful, trusting and strong woman had lifted it off, making him at once more vulnerable and more free.

As the ambulance, lights flashing but no siren, pulled onto the highway, two Colorado State Patrol vehicles pulled in front of Simon's cruiser. "Agent Woolridge?" A silver-haired man in a heavy black coat stepped out of the first vehicle and addressed Simon.

"Yes." Simon straightened and offered his hand.

"Sergeant Nick Schwartz." The older man looked down at Simon's hand, but didn't take it. "Are you all right, sir?"

Simon realized his hands were still covered in blood. He wiped them on his uniform, but it was almost as soiled. "I was delivering a baby," he said, by way of explanation.

Schwartz nodded toward Victor's body. "What happened to him?"

"He's a fugitive I've been pursuing. Victor Krayev, a Russian hit man."

"You take him out?"

"No. He was killed by a man who goes by the name of Daniel Metwater." The real story was too complicated to go into now. "I need you to put a guard on Ms. Matheson at the hospital. She could still be in danger from Metwater."

Schwartz and his partner exchanged looks. "We can do that," Schwartz said. "But we'd like a few more details."

"It's a long story," Simon said.

"This is a story I want to hear," the other man, a trim Hispanic with black-rimmed glasses, said.

"It'll have to wait," Simon said. "I have some things I have to do right now."

"Sir, we'll need you to make a statement," Schwartz said.

But Simon was already in his cruiser with the engine running. "I'll be in touch," he said, and drove away.

He waited to make sure no one had come

after him, then pulled out his phone and dialed Ranger Headquarters. Carmen Redhorse answered. "Simon! What's going on? We were expecting you hours ago."

"I ran into a little trouble. I need to speak with the commander."

"Simon." Graham Ellison's voice held more warmth than Simon had expected. "Are you all right?" the commander asked. "Is Andi all right?"

"She's doing okay. She had her baby—a little girl." He looked down at his hands. "I delivered it." The idea filled him with wonder.

"Good job. Where are you now?"

"I'm still near Fairplay. She and the baby are on their way to Breckenridge in an ambulance."

"Why didn't you go with them?"

"They'll be okay. Victor Krayev is dead, and the local police agreed to put a guard on her."

"Did you kill Victor?"

"No. Metwater did. Victor was sent by the *Bratva* to kill him and to retrieve a key to a safe-deposit box that apparently contains money the Russians think belongs to them."

"So Daniel Metwater shot him?" Graham asked.

"Not Daniel—David. Apparently David Metwater killed Daniel and assumed his brother's identity in an attempt to get away from the Russians. But they learned the truth and came after him anyway."

"You're saying the man who died in Chicago wasn't David, he was Daniel?" Graham asked. "Back up and start over. Slower this time."

So Simon told him the story of the two brothers, one who stole a million dollars from the Russian mob and tried to get away with it by switching identities with his straight-arrow brother. "Apparently, the body was so deteriorated from a week in the water that the chief means of identification was the distinctive tattoo," Simon said. "David, as next of kin, essentially identified the body as himself."

"How did he get around having an autopsy performed, since the body was that of a murder victim?" Ellison asked.

"Maybe he bribed someone?" Simon said. "I don't know. But he somehow convinced authorities to take his identification as final proof of identity, then he had the body cremated."

"And he declared himself so transformed by his brother's death that he turned his back on his old life and hid out in the wilderness with a bunch of followers," Ellison said.

"Except the leopard couldn't completely change his spots," Simon said. "He got greedy. He wanted Andi Metwater's money, and he wanted the million dollars he had hidden away in a safe-deposit box. The *Bratva* hadn't forgotten about that money either though. And they figured out the truth about which brother had really died."

"How did they do that?" Graham asked.

"I don't know. But they found the guy David paid to give his brother the tattoo. Once they knew the truth, they sent Victor to retrieve the key to the safe-deposit box where David had stashed the money, and to exact revenge for trying to double-cross them."

"But Metwater killed him first. And he got away?"

"He would have killed Andi and me if the police hadn't arrived. He got away, and he has the locket that belonged to Michelle's sister. He hid the key to the safe-deposit box in it, though he'll soon find out the key isn't in it now. Andi was afraid to carry it around, once she knew its significance, so she hid it in her uncle's cabin."

"When Metwater finds out, he'll come after Andi again," Graham said.

"Maybe. The local police have agreed to put a guard on her at the hospital. But Metwater strikes me as a smart guy—good at figuring out puzzles. I have a feeling he'll check the cabin first, so I'm headed there now."

"You should wait for backup."

"I should, but if I do that, he'll get away. And I don't want to risk him coming after Andi again. I want this to end now."

"I can't authorize a solo pursuit," Graham said.

"I'm not asking permission, sir. I'm only advising you of what I'm doing."

"Simon."

"He tried to kill the woman I love, and her baby. I'm not going to give him a second chance."

The commander was silent for a long moment. Simon was getting used to those silences—it meant Graham was thinking, coming up with a plan. "I'm going to contact state patrol when I get off the phone and send them after you," he said. "If they get to you before you find Metwater, they'll be under orders to take you with them."

"Fair enough, sir. But tell them not to hurry. I want a piece of this guy."

"Good luck, Simon. But remember that luck will take you only so far."

"I'll remember, sir. And thank you."

He hung up the phone, and gripped the steering wheel with both hands. He wasn't nervous or afraid. His instincts told him he was doing the right thing. Metwater was going to be at the cabin. And Simon was going to be there, too, to take him down.

The Prophet might have thought he had gotten away with murder, but Simon was determined to prove him wrong.

Simon followed the tracks of Metwater's tires all the way down the forest service road that led to the cabin. The snow had stopped and the sun had come out, glinting off ice crystals so that the whole world looked as if it were coated in white sugar.

He passed the turnoff for the cabin and drove a half mile farther, then parked on the side of the road. The tracks he had been following had turned off at the cabin. Either Metwater hadn't expected anyone to follow him or he was so focused on the key—and the million dollars it led to—that he didn't care.

Simon cleaned his hands and drank some water, then began working his way toward the cabin. He would approach it from the back and try to catch Metwater by surprise. The Prophet wouldn't give up without a fight, so Simon would have to use every advantage.

He hadn't gone very far before he was wet to the knees, melting snow soaking into his clothes. Branches caught and tugged at his coat and a crow cawed indignantly overhead. Simon ignored the bird and the wet and kept going, gun drawn, carefully placing each step, yet moving as swiftly as possible.

He heard Metwater before he saw him. The thud of something being dropped was followed by the crash of breaking glass. More thuds and crashes. Once, the Rangers had been called to deal with a bear that had become trapped inside an RV. The bear had destroyed the interior of the trailer before the Rangers succeeded in freeing him. Metwater sounded as if he was wreaking the same kind of havoc. Good. The noise would help cover Simon's approach.

At the edge of the trees behind the cabin, he paused. He detected no movement outside, though the crashing sounds continued inside. He counted to ten, deliberately slowing his breath, then darted forward, to a position to the left of the big back window.

The glass of the window was shattered, a slight breeze stirring the curtains. Simon remembered that Victor had entered the cabin this way when he had tried to kidnap Andi. He waited, listening to the muffled slamming doors and clatter of items falling.

Simon leaned over and looked inside. The mattress was half off the bed, the covers on the floor. All the drawers had been removed from the dresser, the contents scattered. No sign of Metwater—though Simon could hear him in the front of the house.

He climbed in the window and moved toward the source of the commotion, stepping around mounds of winter clothing and tumbled stacks of magazines. At the door to the bedroom, he paused, peering around the jamb.

Metwater was crouched in front of the kitchen sink. He pulled out a small metal toolbox, the red paint scratched, rust showing in spots. He opened the lid and began pawing through the contents, then, with a growl of frustration, upended the whole thing on the floor. Wrenches and screwdrivers bounced across the wood floor, and nails and screws rolled in every direction.

"Ah!" he exclaimed, and picked up something from the floor. The small brass key glinted in the sunlight as he held it aloft.

Simon stepped from the bedroom and leveled his gun at the other man. "David Metwater, you're under arrest," he said.

Metwater froze, then turned slowly toward him, the key still in his hand, his gun tucked into the waistband of his trousers. "It was a mistake to come after me," he said. "You should have quit when you had the chance."

"Lay your gun on the floor and stand up with your hands where I can see them," Simon said.

"Do you know what this key is?" Metwater asked.

"Your gun," Simon said. "Drop it."

"This is the key to a safe-deposit box that contains a million dollars. Money I took from the *Bratva*. Can you imagine the audacity?

No one steals from them and gets away with it. But I did."

"I'm arresting you for the murders of Daniel Metwater and Victor Krayev," Simon said. "You have the right to remain silent."

Metwater sneered. "You don't think I'll come quietly, do you?" he asked. "Not after all I've been through to get here. I'm going to kill you, and then I'm going to find Asteria and kill her. Then no one will know I'm not really Daniel Metwater, the prophet who was persecuted by the authorities."

"Plenty of people know the truth now," Simon said. "Put down your weapon and keep your hands where I can see them."

"Have you ever seen a million dollars?" Metwater asked. "Stacks and stacks of bills. More money than many people will see in a lifetime."

"You are entitled to consult an attorney,"

Simon said. "If you cannot afford one, one will be appointed for you by the court."

"Shut up." Metwater shifted his focus from the key to Simon. "I know my rights. I have been arrested before—or rather, David was arrested. Daniel has a clean record. But we don't have to do this. We can come to an agreement that will satisfy us both."

"I'll only be satisfied when you're behind bars," Simon said.

"Hear me out." Metwater held up the key again. "Let me go and I will give you half of the contents of this box. Half a million dollars. Think of that."

"Your words are worthless to me," Simon said.

"You think I will cheat you, but no. Half a million dollars, Officer. Cops don't get paid that much, do they? Think of what you could do with half a million dollars."

Half a million would build a new wing on

the orphanage his aunt managed on the border. It would buy supplies and medicine for the clinic his uncle ran. It could fund a scholarship in memory of his father and mother.

"Put down your gun," Simon said.

"Of course." Metwater drew the gun from his waistband, extended it in front of him, and fired.

Simon dove for the floor, the bullet thudding into the wall behind him. His own shot caught Metwater square in the chest. He fired a second time, and a third, until Metwater dropped his weapon and sank to the floor. The brass key clattered on the wood and came to rest in a beam of sunlight by the table.

Sirens whined in the distance, moving closer. Simon rose to his knees, heart pounding, his breathing coming hard. He was still sitting that way when the state patrol officers burst in, guns drawn. Simon laid his pistol aside.

"He's dead," he said. "It's over."

ANDI SMILED DOWN at the baby in her arms, who looked up at her with wonder in her eyes. The nurses had dressed her in a pink onesie and a little pink hat, and wrapped her in a flowered flannel blanket. All the trauma surrounding her birth hadn't harmed her. The doctors had pronounced mother and baby both healthy, and free to go home as soon as all the paperwork had been processed.

Home. Andi had no idea where that was now. With the Prophet still on the loose, would she need to go to the safe house? And then what? Her twenty-fifth birthday had passed, so she supposed she was a rich woman. She could buy a house—one with a sunny room for a nursery, and a backyard where her little girl could play when she was older. But the idea didn't excite her. A house by herself sounded so lonely. Empty.

A knock on the door interrupted her contemplation. She looked up and Simon stepped into the room. Her heart beat wildly at the sight of him. He was back in uniform, his hair neatly combed, his face close shaven—this was the Simon she remembered from all his visits to the Family's compound in the woods. Except that this time he carried a bouquet of flowers—red daisies and orange mums and purple lilies spilling from a twist of green tissue. He wasn't smiling as he walked toward the bed, his eyes focused first on the baby, then on her. Dark eyes that made her melt a little inside. But right now they also made her want to cry. She was afraid of what he would say to her—and what he wouldn't say.

She spoke first, rushing to get the words out. "I'm so glad you're okay," she said. "I've been worried." As the hours passed when he didn't come to see her, she had imagined everything from him being killed to him deciding he never wanted to see her again.

"You didn't have to worry about me," he said.

"What happened?" she asked. "The Prophet?"

"He's dead. He won't have a chance to hurt you again."

His face was grim, and she wondered if he had been the one to kill Metwater. But she wouldn't ask. She didn't want that kind of ugliness in this room—not now.

Simon stared again at the baby. "Is she okay?" he asked. "Are you okay?"

"We're both doing great. Would you like to hold her?"

She half expected him to say no, but instead, he laid the bouquet at the foot of the bed and carefully took the baby in his arms. She looked impossibly tiny there—and so right. Andi's eyes stung and she swallowed past a lump in her throat.

"She's beautiful," he said, and looked up at her.

"I named her Caroline, after my mother."

"It's a beautiful name." He looked down at

the baby, who stared back up at him, as if trying to figure him out. "She's so tiny," he said.

"You look just right, holding her," she said.

"I don't know anything about babies," he said.

"Neither do I." *We can learn together*, she thought, but was afraid to say it.

"I should tell you what happened after I left you," he said, his eyes still on the baby.

"You don't have to," she said.

"I want to." He hesitated, then added, "I think I need to."

"All right."

"I went back to your uncle's cabin. I figured once Metwater discovered the key was no longer in the locket, he would go there to look."

"Was he there?"

"Yes. He had found the key. He tried to bribe me, offering me half of the money if I would let him go."

"But you turned him down."

"Yes." He folded the blanket back from little Caroline's face. "He tried to shoot me and I shot back. He's dead now."

"Oh." Was it wrong that the news made her feel relieved? "What will happen to the money now?"

"That will be up to the authorities in Chicago. They'll have to figure out which bank issued that key and where the box is located. The money will probably end up going back to the government."

"I'm so glad you're all right," she said again. "I can't thank you enough for everything you've done. If you hadn't been there when I went into labor, I don't know what I would have done."

"Don't thank me. I didn't do anything special."

"I wouldn't have made it without you. Caroline wouldn't have made it."

"Don't look at me like I'm a saint," he said,

his expression angry. "I'm not. I'm not going to save you or be as good as you want me to be. I know good people—truly good people. My aunt is a nun who runs an orphanage on the border. My uncle is a doctor who gives away thousands of dollars' worth of medical care every week. Both my parents died because they stood up to help others. I'm nothing compared to them."

"Stop it!" It was her turn to be angry now. "I know you think I'm a naive, starry-eyed girl," she said. "And I was that once. But I've done a lot of growing up in the last few weeks—mostly in the last few days with you. I know you're not perfect—you're grumpy and reticent and impatient and you snore. But those things don't matter to me. Because I see beneath all that stuff you use to keep other people from getting too close. I see it because I used to be that way too."

"You were never grumpy, and you don't snore."

"No, but I know how to keep people at a distance by remaining aloof. They think it's because you believe you're better than them, but I know it's because you think you'll never be good enough. You can't let anyone get close enough to find that out." She leaned toward him. "But we let each other get close, Simon. We couldn't help it. And what I found out is that we're a lot more alike than you give us credit for."

His gaze met hers, pinning her in place. "All I want to know is, did you mean it when you said you love me?"

"Yes. Too much."

"You can't love someone too much," he said.

"It feels like it, when even the idea of you being taken from me rips me in half."

"I'm not going anywhere." He leaned toward her, the baby between them, and his lips met hers, a kiss of such sweet tenderness that she felt tears well once more.

She opened her eyes and found him looking at her. "I'm not going to let you go," he said.

"Good. Because I'm not going anywhere. Except home with you, if you'll have me."

"I'm not an easy person to live with."

"I'm not expecting easy. Just someone I can count on." She didn't need a man with all the answers, just one who wouldn't let her down. Simon had proved he was that person—not a prophet or a politician or a celebrity, but a good man who would do his best for her, and made her want to do her best for him.

"Let's go home," he said. "We have a new life to get started on."

"I can't wait," she said. "This is going to be the best one yet."

* * * * *

LET'S TALK

Romance

For exclusive extracts, competitions and special offers, find us online:

f facebook.com/millsandboon

◎ @millsandboonuk

𝕐 @millsandboon

Or get in touch on 0844 844 1351*

For all the latest titles coming soon,
visit millsandboon.co.uk/nextmonth